ALICE

JUDITH HERMANN
Translated from the German by
Margot Bettauer Dembo

THE CLERKENWELL PRESS

Published in Great Britain in 2011 by
CLERKENWELL PRESS
An imprint of Profile Books Ltd
Pine Street
Exmouth Market
London EC1R oJH
www.profilebooks.com

First published by Fischer Verlag, Germany
Copyright © Judith Hermann, 2010, 2011
Translation copyright © Margot Bettauer Dembo, 2011

10 9 8 7 6 5 4 3 2 1

Printed and bound in Italy by
L.E.G.O. S.p.a. Lavis

The moral right of the author has been asserted.

Typeset by MacGuru Ltd in Granjon
info@macguru.org.uk

A CIP catalogue record for this book is available from the British Library.

ISBN 978 1 84668 529 3
eISBN 978 1 84765 747 3

ALICE

Contents

I

Misha

But Misha didn't die. Not during the night from Monday to Tuesday, nor the night from Tuesday to Wednesday; perhaps he would die Wednesday evening or later that night. Alice thought she had heard it said that most people die at night. The doctors weren't saying anything any more; they shrugged their shoulders and held out their empty, disinfected hands. There's nothing more we can do. Sorry.

And so Alice, Maja, and Maja's child had to look for another place to stay. Another holiday apartment, because Misha couldn't die. Their present holiday apartment was too small. They really needed at least two bedrooms, one for Maja and the child and the other for Alice, as well as a living room with a TV for the evenings, a halfway decently equipped kitchen to take care of the child's needs, a bath with a bathtub. A garden? Or a window with a view of something beautiful.

In the hospital, Misha was wearing a hospital gown printed all over with blue diamonds. He was reduced to skin and bones, a skeleton; but his hands were as they had always been – they were also soft and warm. On his bedside table there was nothing now except a bottle of mineral water and a sipper cup. Though by now he'd even stopped drinking water.

Alice packed her overnight bag. A nightgown, three T-shirts, three sweaters, a pair of slacks, underwear, a book. She sat down on the wicker sofa among the cushions and rolled a green plastic ball with a little bell tinkling inside it across the tiled tabletop towards the child. The child was already able to stand at the low living-room table, proudly, holding on to the tabletop with both hands. She didn't react to the ball, but emphatically repeated the word 'rabbit' several times in a row. Very clearly. Maja was on the phone with the owner of a holiday apartment at the other end of town. Cheaper. Three rooms. With a garden. A washing machine too, yes, of course. No further from the hospital than this one-room place with its fake forsythia in a vase on the built-in cupboard, the framed photo above the TV showing the sun setting into an empty lake, the folding bed on which Alice had slept in front of the built-in cupboard, the double bed in the corner, and the wicker sofa pushed to the window. The curtains were drawn aside and the view was of a supermarket car park, vehicles coming and going, and people pushing brimful shopping trolleys.

… in the Catholic hospital, Maja was saying on the phone. My husband is in the Catholic hospital. She was sitting on the edge of the bed, her head cradled in her hand, her face turned away. Alice gazed at her back. Now the child had decided to take the plastic ball after all, lifting it up and shaking it hard, listening to the little bell with a rapt expression on her face.

We're moving, Alice said to the child. We're moving to another place. It's going to be really nice there, you'll see. There's a bathtub. A garden – we can go outside every morning. Trees. A lawn. Maybe rabbits, we'll see, maybe we can catch one.

The child didn't reply. She looked at Alice, a long look full of mysterious significance. A clear drop of spit trembled on her little chin. She was Misha's child and looked a lot like her father.

The way things had turned out, Misha now lay dying in Zweibrücken – Two Bridges. The name sounded poetic to Alice, but it presented a distorted image, because for the dying man there was only one bridge, if any at all. For whom was the second one? Zweibrücken turned out to be the end of an odyssey that had led from one hospital to another – and then in the end and by coincidence it happened to be a Catholic hospital in a town far from home where Misha now lay dying. He might have joked about it if he'd had the strength. But he no longer did. He had cancer and was on morphine, was nearly gone. Alice wasn't even sure whether the sound he made when she sat by his bed and put his hand in hers was intended as an expression of pain or acceptance. The doctors, who had withdrawn from the case a week ago, still hovered in the background out of courtesy. Now and then, one of them would come by and pretend to take his temperature or feel his pulse. For days they had predicted his death, but he didn't die. Kept breathing, in and out. In and out. In and out. That was all.

Maja was putting a fresh nappy on the child. On the double bed. The child was beautiful, her skin soft and white. On her back there was a heart-shaped birthmark, a mark of distinction. Alice sat on the wicker sofa and watched as Maja changed the child's nappy, holding both little legs in her left hand and gently raising the child by her little feet.

We'll take a taxi, Maja said. Could you call for one. In ten minutes.

OK, Alice said.

They didn't talk much. Sometimes more, sometimes less; it wasn't awkward. The night before they had sat next to each other in silence, watching the child eat pizza. For quite a while. Alice got up and washed the last of the dishes, two coffee mugs, two plates, the small bowl from which the child had eaten a lunch of plain yogurt with banana slices. Please pack up the things from the refrigerator, too, Maja said. She told the child to lie still. Don't move – just for a moment.

There were eggs, fish, tomatoes and a piece of butter in the refrigerator. And fennel tea, potatoes, apples, and pears. Plus three bottles of beer and a bottle of wine. In the pot on the stove there were sterilised teats and the child's feeding bottle. Alice unfolded two bright yellow bags, feeling unduly helpless – she wanted to do everything just so.

Then the landlord was standing at the door. He had knocked inaudibly, just wanted to check whether everything was all right. Alice counted some notes into his outstretched hand; she saw no reason to lie to him. No. We're not leaving town, we're just moving; this place is really too small for us. But otherwise everything's fine. Thank you very much. No, it will still take a while. It's not over yet. The doctors say he's very strong. The landlord smiled, a crooked, ineffectual smile; he looked quite awkward, but what else could he do.

Where will you be going?

To the outskirts of town, Maja called out from the bed. There's supposed to be a garden there; that's better for the child. But thanks for everything. Thank you very much all the same.

Maja and the child had been in Zweibrücken for ten days. They had come by plane; it was the child's first time flying, and she didn't cry at take-off or landing. Maja had booked the holiday apartment from Berlin, had told the landlord that she wasn't coming to Zweibrücken on holiday. Did anyone ever go to Zweibrücken on holiday? The landlord didn't have an answer. Forty euros a night for the room, the forsythia, and a bath with a shower. On their fourth day there the child had started crying inconsolably as soon as they were on the street leading to the hospital, and that's when Maja had phoned Alice.

Can you come? Misha is dying. Don't you want to see him once more? I need someone to look after the child; she no longer wants to go to the hospital with me.

Alice was tempted to ask, Do you think Misha wants to see me? Don't you think it might be too much for him? But how could Maja know whether Misha wanted to see Alice or not.

Instead she had asked, What's the matter with the child?

Maja had thought for a moment and then she said, The child no longer reacts to Misha as if he were a person. I can't take her into his hospital room any more. But I want to be with him. You understand that, don't you?

Alice left Berlin the next day. She barely knew Maja. She knew Misha. Of course she wanted to see him one more time; what kind of a question was that. There had been times when she thought she couldn't live if she couldn't see Misha's face any more. She had often told him that, and each time he had laughed good-naturedly. But she also thought he would die while the train in which she sat was rolling through the desolate and ugly landscape; she considered herself so important that she assumed Misha would die because she was coming and before she could be at his side.

In spite of that, she had left for Zweibrücken. Misha did

not die. Not while she was sitting on the train, reading a newspaper, falling asleep and waking up again, drinking coffee, eating a tart apple, looking through the window, crying, going to the toilet, and twice changing her seat. Seeing signs in everything and misinterpreting them. Misha didn't die, not when she arrived in the town and Maja and the child picked her up at the station, not when they embraced and Maja said, We can cry later. Misha didn't die the first night that Alice took care of the child while Maja went to the hospital, nor the second, and before the third night they had decided to move.

They were standing on the pavement, waiting for the taxi. The pushchair was collapsed. The bags of food from the refrigerator sat next to Alice's overnight bag and Maja's suitcase. Earthly goods. Every word suddenly had a second meaning. The pavement was narrow, cars rushed by, raising fountains of rainwater behind them. Nobody was out walking. The taxi didn't come. Maja, holding the child in her arms, rocked her a while, then she passed her to Alice. Alice took the child, afraid she might put up a fight, but the child didn't resist her, just looked so very serious. Alice held the child in one arm, supporting part of the weight on her hip, the way you hold children. The closeness of the little face, framed by a fluffy pink pompom hat, embarrassed her. The child smelled of baby, of milk, and mashed carrots; her blue eyes were huge and shiny. Alice had to look away; she gazed up and down the street. What a place. The street crossed over the motorway, ran through a park where dishevelled ducks swam in a stagnant pond, then on to the desolate centre of town and up to the hospital – a walk of twenty minutes with the pushchair and the child who, just learning to walk, wanted to walk all the time, but never straight ahead, rather this way and that way. She was learning to walk in spite of everything and precisely because of it all. Maja had been taking this route for a week now. There. And back. The child had thrown soggy biscuits to the ducks. The ducks barely noticed. It was cold, the middle of October, not golden. The child on Alice's arm turned her head and saw what Alice saw. Rain and grey houses. Nothing that they might have pointed out to each other.

Maybe I ought to call the taxi again, Alice said, but Maja didn't react, which probably meant that there was no need to call again. Alice found that Maja often spoke by saying nothing, expressing herself clearly with silence. In different circumstances Alice might have objected to this silence. But Maja was Misha's wife. They had a child together, and once Misha was dead, Maja would be his widow. The affair between Misha and Alice had happened too long ago for her to claim any rights whatsoever. Just an anecdote but, Alice thought, if it weren't for that anecdote, I wouldn't be in Zweibrücken now. And yet, my being here doesn't change the fact that Misha is dying.

The taxi pulled up at the kerb. The driver made a face; he didn't feel like climbing out, getting his feet wet, packing all their stuff into the boot – the pushchair, the suitcase, the overnight bag, the bags of food. He got out. Maja

took the child from Alice and smiled at the driver. Alice
got into the front seat. In the back the driver fiddled nerv-
ously with the child's seat. Maja was holding the child in
her lap, still smiling. Then they drove off. Nice windscreen
wipers, music on the radio, the regional station, idle chatter,
a gong, and then pop songs. Looking out of the window.
Driving down the street, crossing the motorway – the sign-
posts, upcoming exits were all clearly visible, drawing one
to distant places, the possibility of getting away from Zweibrücken again. Let's beat it, disappear, clear out, skedaddle
– it was a language that was suddenly no longer appropriate
here. They drove past the park; the hospital whisked by,
seven storeys with twenty windows each – the third from
the left on the seventh floor was the window of the room
where Misha lay in bed, breathing in and breathing out.
The door to his room always ajar, and his breathing so loud
you could already hear it as you walked out of the lift.

You'll be shocked when you see him, Maja had said the
first time Alice went to the hospital. And she had been.

Alice didn't look up at the hospital window. They drove
uphill briefly, leaving the centre of town, then through a
wooded area and into a housing development. The cab
driver had a terrible cough. Number twelve, Maja said from
the back seat. Alice paid, didn't ask for a receipt. The driver
took their things out of the boot, mumbling to himself as he
did. Then he drove off. Alice, Maja and the child stood in
the street looking at the house – a small, new, white house
with a conservatory in which huge azaleas were pressing
against the fogged-up panes. A rustic witch sitting on a

straw broom hung outside the stained-glass panel set into the front door, swinging and rustling in the wind. Alice thought she knew what the doorbell would sound like. The air was brisk. Suddenly they could smell the rain, the wet soil, the damp leaves.

Alice had been at the hospital that morning. After breakfast. One of the doctors had said, There are people who find it easier to die alone; let him be by himself for a little while, don't worry. Misha had been alone from one o'clock at night till ten o'clock in the morning, nine hours during which he had been breathing and did not die.

That morning Alice sat at Misha's bedside until noon. First on one side of the bed, then on the other. The room was utilitarian, fitted cupboards, a sink, the door to the toilet, a bare area of painted linoleum where a second bed had stood in which another patient had been lying. Some days ago the nurses had pushed him elsewhere, without giving any reasons. To some other place.

Sitting on the right side of the bed, Alice had her back to the window that looked out on the city and a distant range of hills. Sitting on the left-hand side of the bed, she'd be next to the IV drip stand for the morphine, but leaning back against the wall unit, she could look out of the window and see the hills when she could no longer bear to look at Misha. To look at his face. Misha slept with his eyes open. The entire time. Like a plant, he had turned to the light, towards the grey but bright day – his body, his head, his arms and hands turned towards the window. In spite of the open eyes he looked as though he were sleeping, but perhaps it was something quite different, this state he was in, anaesthetised by morphine, flooded by images, or by nothing at all any more. He had sighed, often and deeply. Sometimes Alice would take his hand, which was warm and so very familiar. The door to the room was slightly ajar, the squeaking of the nurses' shoes was comforting – the ringing of the telephone at the nurses' station, the rumbling of the lift, the whispering and laughter, a constant bustle, the food trolley rolling past the room. Now and then one of the nuns would come in. An old, wrinkled nun came by often; Alice thought she came on her account rather than because of Misha.

Everything all right?

Yes, so far.

The nun had stopped at the foot of the bed and, holding on to the metal bar, had gazed at Misha with her head cocked. Interested. His mouth was open, the gums black, his unseeing eyes turned towards the window. The nun had looked at Alice and asked what sort of man he had been.

How do you mean? Alice had asked, sitting up; she had been slumped down in the chair leaning against the wall unit.

Do you mean what was his profession?

The nun had lifted her hands casually and dropped them again, giving the bed a jolt. She said, Well, how did he spend his life? What did he do?

They had both looked at Misha, and Alice thought the nun would never know what Misha had been like, how he had looked, how he talked, cursed, and smiled – how he had lived his life. She saw only the dying man. Was she missing something?

Hesitantly Alice said, Well, I'd say he was a magician. A conjurer – do you know what I mean? He could do all sorts of tricks, pull rabbits out of a hat, juggling. Mind reading. But he always let you look at his cards. He always wanted to show you his cards. I can't explain it.

The nun said, I thought it was something like that. Her tone of voice was neutral; it could have been agreement or scorn, hard to tell. She said, Well, it won't be much longer. Once their features get so sharp, it doesn't take much longer. Then she left the room.

The door to the small, white house opened by itself, they didn't have to ring. Probably everybody here had seen everything, standing behind the curtains of their terrace doors, in the shaded corners of their living rooms on this quiet, peaceful street. They had all seen the taxi stop, had seen them get out. A blonde and a dark-haired woman and a small child wearing a little pink hat. And all three with dark rings under their eyes. A suitcase, bags, and a push-chair. The door opened by itself, the owners came out of the house. Welcome, they extended their arms. A fat woman and a fat man, older people, the age of Maja's parents, Alice's parents. Alice was older than Maja, and Misha wasn't that young any more either. Alice had always thought he would outlive her. Would outlive them all. Misha would always be there. That's what she had thought. She wouldn't have been able to say why she thought so. Perhaps it was an expression of her love, something timeless. Standing in front of the house, the food bags in one hand and the overnight bag in the other, and Maja next to her with the child on her arm and all those little things at the edges of the picture – ornamental spheres in flower beds, the earth already dug up, green grass, a white clay turtle – Alice felt a trembling in her knees that threatened to get out of control but then went away again. The woman had a big bosom, was wearing violet-tinted glasses; she was incredibly cordial, not quite natural. The man, always hovering a little distance behind her, his hands rough and worn, his handshake firm; his tracksuit bottoms were filthy and there were extensive scars on both sides of his broad, shaven skull, as if his head had once been held in a clamp. It looked peculiar, but then everything seemed peculiar, had to be accepted for what it was. Alice carried her bag into the front garden and up the broken paving stones of the front path while the child on Maja's arm kept saying, Rabbit. Rabbit. Rabbit. As if to calm everyone.

The holiday apartment was in the basement. The woman explained that it had been their own apartment; they had finished it with their own hands. The man said nothing, just smiled. Their daughter used to live upstairs with the grandchildren and they themselves, downstairs. Then the daughter and the grandchildren had moved out, had gone away to another city. Now they were living upstairs again, so they wanted to rent out the basement flat; it would be a shame not to. The woman gave this verbose explanation as if to apologise; she spoke in a heavy dialect, and Alice understood only half of what she was saying, but when all was said and done, it didn't matter who had lived in the apartment or when or why. Alice walked behind Maja who was following the woman who had immediately taken the child into her arms, had taken off the little pink hat, and was now carrying the child as though it were her own. They all trooped down the stairs. First, the woman with the now silent, serious child, then Maja, then Alice, then the man, who was carrying the suitcase, overnight bag and bags of food. Very helpful. He was right behind Alice, breathing heavily.

The house was built on a slope. Only half the apartment was below street level, and at the back it led out to the garden. At first glance everything seemed fine. It had a certain cosiness – a large room with a wall of fitted kitchen cabinets and built-in appliances and in the middle a table of light-coloured wood; there were shelves filled with cookbooks and bric-a-brac, a television set, and a corner sofa; leading off from this room there was first one bedroom and then another, both with beds in them, and the bathroom with a tub and a washing machine.

But on second glance it wasn't quite all right – small details, here and there. Maybe these people had moved upstairs only yesterday, hadn't taken everything up with them, had left behind their personal stuff: framed photos, a collection of liquor bottles , crumpled magazines, and half-finished knitting. In the bathroom, a row of cheap shampoo and shower-gel bottles on the rim of the bathtub. And children's toys – immediately discovered by Maja's child. Clothes in the wardrobe, slippers under the coat rack. There really was nothing to object to, everything was comfortable otherwise, but it was also very intimate and personal, an additional burden. Alice felt a twinge of nausea, but then she remembered the depressing décor of the other holiday apartment, where everything had been practical but nothing more. The child was very happy here. She immediately swept all the bric-a-brac off the shelves and pulled down the tablecloth, emptied a washing-powder box full of building blocks, and rattled the refrigerator door. The woman cooed and laughed, trying to reassure Maja, who kept apologising for the child's behaviour. The woman ran hither and thither showing off everything: the electric kettle, the coffee maker, the electric blinds, the television set, video recorder, bed sheets, keys. On the key ring, a tiny witch on a wire broom.

Alice stood at the window in the kitchen, gazing out at the garden. A porch swing on the terrace was covered with a tarpaulin. Four white chairs surrounded a plastic table and in the middle, a furled patio umbrella. The trees were already nearly bare. Wilted dahlias, asters, sunflowers, a pergola, and red grapes. A nice view of other gardens up and down the hillside, then the first city houses, and far to the left, there was the hospital – a long rectangle with many windows. Too far away for her to identify the window of Misha's room, but close enough to know: Misha's there. And we're here.

Alice saw it and felt that if she didn't immediately show Maja she would be guilty of a betrayal. But she kept it to herself a moment longer. Maja was busy with the woman and the child in one of the bedrooms. It sounded as if the child was jumping up and down on the bed, squealing with delight. Alice turned away from the window to look at the stainless-steel sink, at the shelf above it. Plastic containers of herbs and spices, half full, marjoram, rosemary, multi-coloured pepper, all of it a little messy, a sticky film on the jar tops; the sink wasn't entirely clean either. She turned on the tap to test it and shut it off again. Then the man was standing behind her. He put his arms around her, his hands on her hips, pulling her towards him, holding her like that; then he pushed her to one side and let go. He said, The tablets for the dishwasher are under the sink, and he gestured vaguely downwards.

Alice said, Oh, thanks, I'm sure we'll be using them. She raised her hand to touch the back of her neck, astonished, and slowly turned to face him. As though it were possible to obliterate what had happened. To obliterate that embrace.

He shook his head. He smiled out of the window and said, There's no need for thanks. You're having a hard time. You're having a really hard time.

Then he stepped aside as though he were already standing at the newly dug grave. He retreated with feigned modesty, his eyes cast down, still shaking his head. His wife came hurrying out of the bedroom carrying a pile of lilac-coloured sheets and pillowcases in her arms, red patches on her face.

We'll make the beds ourselves, Maja called out from the bedroom. Please don't go to any trouble; we can manage by ourselves, really. The woman looked at her husband, then at Alice, but not back again. Alice went over to her and took the sheets. Are you sure? the woman asked. Yes, Alice said without knowing what she was supposed to be sure of.

Maja came into the kitchen-living room; she leaned against the bedroom doorway. The door frame was cobbled together from old beams, an imitation of permanence. The child crawling behind her on all fours now pulled herself up on Maja's hand and twined her little arms around Maja's knee. Wearing only a shirt and tights, and hiccupping softly, she looked heartbreakingly tired.

Alice said, we're really glad to be here. It's lovely; the garden alone – she searched for a gesture and found none – but it didn't matter at all. The man and the woman finally left, finally dragged themselves upstairs. Heavy animals, shy and curious; they went up the stairs backwards, kept calling out reassurances, consolations, directions – until they disappeared from view, the man first. Maja pushed the door shut with the palm of her hand; then leaned her head against the glass pane.

That afternoon Alice went to see Misha once more. For an hour, while Maja and the child slept. She left the development, then walked along the street into town, downhill through the woods. It was no longer raining, just misty and cold. She had her hands in her jacket pockets and a scarf around her neck. It was peaceful in the hospital. A mosaic in the entrance hall showed a monk with his arms spread in a blessing under a sky of thousands of tiny blue tiles. Next to it a coffee machine was humming. Alice walked past a bulletin board full of passport photos of the hospital's doctors, nurses, and nuns. She could have looked for the face of the little wrinkled nun who had asked what sort of man Misha had been. Could have looked for her name, but something kept her from doing it.

She took the lift up to the seventh floor and could hear Misha's breathing as the doors slid open. The door to his room was slightly ajar. Misha lay there as though he hadn't moved in all the hours she'd been gone. On his back, arms extended to the left and right, face turned to the fading light, mouth open, eyes open. Alice placed the chair she had pushed against the table that morning next to his bed again. She sat down and cautiously said his name. He didn't react. Still, Alice had the feeling that he knew she was there. Whether it mattered to him that she was there, whether it was a strain for him – *that* she didn't know. There was no longer anything to which he could have reacted. Whatever there had once been was gone. All the things that had once existed between him and her were gone too. Nothing left. It was all over; she could say goodbye now. Nothing but the pure, shining present. Alice kissed Misha, as she hadn't kissed him during his lifetime. She knew that he would never have put up with that kind of kiss were he still conscious.

They ate together that evening, Alice, Maja, and the child.

At the table of light-coloured wood, Maja and the child sitting on one side, Alice on the other. Fish and potatoes. The plates with pictures of yellow baby chicks, the glasses with flowers on them. Maja had done the cooking; she cooked with little salt, nothing fancy, a sort of biblical meal; you could call it bland or plain; the child seemed to like it.

Did you eat together often? Alice asked.

Now and then it was possible to ask a question, and Maja would answer, or vice versa, if Maja asked, Alice would answer. But it didn't go beyond that. Questions and answers don't make a conversation. And that's how things stood, Alice thought. A focused emptiness.

Yes, Maja said. Not in the beginning, but later on, we did. When we were living together. Misha liked rice.

Oh, Alice said.

She had seen Misha only rarely this past year, had never visited him in the apartment where he lived with Maja. Actually she hadn't known anything about the child, and wouldn't have wanted to. A different Misha? Maybe not.

With the palm of her hand the child batted once resolutely at the plate with the mashed potatoes and fish. Maja took the tiny hand and wiped it gently with a towel, each of the five little fingers individually. The child watched, nodding. After the fish, there was plain yogurt without honey. And lukewarm fennel tea. The child drank the tea from her bottle, which she could already hold by herself. She was sitting in Maja's lap, looking intently at Alice while she drank.

Well, Maja said, time to go to bed. She carefully set the

child on her feet, waiting till she had found her balance. Then she began to clear the table and said, If Misha gets better, if his temperature doesn't go up again or something, we could order an ambulance next week. Go home, to Berlin. I want him back home. Misha wants that too. He wants to go home.

She rinsed the plates in the sink and put them into the dishwasher, having found the detergent tablets on her own. She moved around the kitchen matter-of-factly and confidently. No hesitation. Maja didn't shy away from anything; nor did anything seem to disgust her. She wiped the table and switched on the kettle.

She said, Was his temperature up today?

Then, squatting in front of the dishwasher, she briefly studied the buttons and symbols, pushed the door of the machine shut, and turned one of the knobs firmly to the right. Soft gushing sounds. Did he have a fever today?

No, Alice said. She returned the child's dreamy gaze, grateful for her neutral quiet. That morning, a pale young nurse had anxiously and awkwardly felt for Misha's pulse and had taken his temperature with a digital thermometer, flinching as if someone had yelled something into her ear at the soft sound – like the chirp of a cricket – that the thermometer made. She then entered some made-up, shaky numbers on a chart and hurried out of the room. The nurse seemed afraid Misha might die while she was taking his temperature. A sudden drop in temperature. Tumbling digital numbers. Plunging towards zero. Alice had the feeling that the nurse's touch, her fingers searching for a pulse on his wrist and then on his neck, had caused Misha pain; after that Alice no longer held his hand in hers.

She said, No, he didn't have a fever. Then she got up and said, Let me clear away the rest. I can do it.

You always use so much water, Maja said. You just let the water run when you're doing dishes, I've noticed that before. Misha used to do that, too. But I cured him of it.

Maja put the child to bed. In the room with the big matrimonial bed in front of the mirrored wardrobe. Lots of blankets and pillows. Alice sat at the table in the kitchen, listening.

Where's the rabbit?

Where's the rabbit?

Here's the rabbit. Here it is.

The child's laughter turned to exhausted crying. Maja hummed, snatches of lullabies, *Morgen früh, wenn Gott will, wirst du wieder geweckt – If God will thou shalt wake, when the morning doth break* ... Now go to sleep. Sleep. Then it was quiet. Alice drank some fennel tea, soundlessly setting her cup down on the tabletop, a kind of meditation. After a while Maja came out of the bedroom, gently pulling the door not quite shut behind her. She sat down on the other side of the table, took a sip of tea, and, like Alice, gazed through the patio door into the dark garden. The glass pane was like a mirror.

Did he say anything to you? Maja asked.

No, Alice said. He was sleeping, the entire time. He scarcely moved. Sighed sometimes, heavily. Nothing else.

Maja nodded. She said, Well, then, I'll be off now. I think I'd better comb my hair.

Alice said nothing. Maja washed her face in the bathroom, combed her hair; she put on a different sweater, grey with green stripes, fluffy, soft wool; it was like going out in reverse, Alice thought.

You look beautiful, she said.

Maja did look beautiful. With those distinct dark rings under the eyes, slender, pale, and tired; her hair firmly combed back off her face and pinned up. A pulsating, dark glow all around her. They went back into the bedroom and together looked at the child. She was sleeping soundly in a sleeping bag patterned with baby lambs. Lying on her back, her little arms extended in complete surrender, clutching the ear of a soft-toy rabbit in her left fist.

Call me if she wakes up and won't stop crying, Maja said. Otherwise I'll be back around midnight, we'll see.

Yes, Alice said. I'll wait for you; I'll wait up till you come.

Alice escorted Maja to the door. They didn't turn on the light, tiptoed up the stairs. The door to the couple's apartment was slightly ajar; through the gap came the noises of the TV – loud applause and the glib, cynical voice of a game-show host. The hallway was cold. It smelled of supper, washing powder, and unfamiliar habits. Alice touched the handle of the front door and for a moment felt sure it would be locked. But the door opened. The evening air as overwhelming as if they hadn't been outside for months. The light in the hallway went on, the woman was standing behind Maja; she wore a tracksuit but no shoes.

Going out so late?

Yes, Maja said. I'm going to the hospital. I want to visit my husband. I haven't been to see him all day.

The woman grimaced as if she'd been stung, as if something had suddenly caused her pain. She had completely forgotten Maja's husband.

Oh, I'll drive you there.

No, thank you, not necessary, Maja said, smiling politely.

Yes, yes, the woman said. Come on, I'll drive you there; this is no place to be walking around in the dark.

She wouldn't take no for an answer, disappeared into her apartment as though sucked in by the blue light of the TV, said something to her husband; he said something to her, all of it drowned out by the noise of the game show. Maja rolled her eyes. Alice didn't know what to say. The woman came back; now she was wearing shoes and a heavy cardigan. She pulled the cardigan down over her broad hips and held up the car key.

Come on. Let's go.

All right, Maja said, see you soon. She briefly touched Alice's arm, then disappeared behind the woman into the front yard.

Alice closed the front door. She felt dizzy. From the couple's apartment came the same blue-cave illumination, the TV spitting out hellish laughter. She went back downstairs, into the basement apartment, locking the door behind her. The door had a frosted glass pane set into a wooden frame. Alice went into the bathroom, opened the window above the tub, a window facing the street. She could hear the car engine start, the car driving out of the driveway, turning, setting off down the street, getting fainter; then it was quiet.

Twenty minutes to walk to the hospital, twenty minutes back again. By car, five minutes. Traffic lights. Traffic at the intersection. A few scraps of conversation. Possibly the woman would decide to go in, too, for whatever reason, she just might. Then five minutes to drive back. Fifteen minutes, all in all, one long, eternal quarter hour. Alice stood in the bathroom and listened. She counted the seconds, starting at one hundred, counting down, was almost sure and yet was still surprised when she heard him. The seventy-fifth second. He came out of the apartment upstairs, did something or other at the front door. Then came down the stairs, clop, clop, clop, his feet in slippers. He turned the corner in the hall, knowing his way, no need for the light. Alice quietly left the bathroom and saw him on the other side of the frosted glass, his lumpy, heavy body. He was listening, listening just as she was. Then he knocked on the wooden door frame.

Alice pulled her plaited hair tight with both hands. Tugged the sleeves of her sweater down over her wrists. Should she open the door or not? Should she open the door or talk to him through the locked door? Show her fear or hide it? Fear of what, exactly? She cut short the stream of crazy thoughts, turned the key, and opened the door.

Yes?

He stood there with that scarred skull and his grey sweater over his fat stomach and those incredibly dirty tracksuit bottoms. He gave off a distinct, sour smell. You don't have to lock the door here, he said.

Oh, Alice said. Her heart was beating fast. She could hardly understand him. She said, What's the matter?

He was smiling now, in a knowing, explicit way. Just wanted to see if you've got everything you need. That's what he said, if Alice understood him right.

Do you have everything you need?

He looked at Alice, her body, from the toes up, still smiling, deliberately and calmly. Alice knew what he meant, and he knew that she knew. Maybe in a figurative sense both of them might not mean the same thing, but in a direct sense they did.

Actually, I don't have any of the things I need, Alice thought. None of them. She said, Thanks, I have everything I need. We have everything, really. Thank you very much.

He thrust himself one heavy step forward and looked past her into his old apartment. Heard the familiar whispering of the dishwasher. Maybe it all seemed different to him now, what with all of Alice's, Maja's, and the child's things in it. Alice's jacket hanging on the coat rack. And the child's soft, tiny shoe on the floor under the table and next to it the green plastic ball – all of it dipped in sadness; he could see how different it was.

Alice let him look. She looked too. She waited, knowing that it didn't matter what her answer had been. He had ten minutes, fifteen at most – in that time anything was possible. But she didn't come towards him, that made him hesitate, and the sadness repelled him, like an illness.

Alice said, Well, then, good night.

He still hesitated.

She said, Good night, again.

He retreated. Clop, clop, back up the stairs. Stopping before the last step – maybe she'd call him back. Alice wondered what Misha would have expected her to do. She didn't have a clue. Holding her hand to her mouth, she listened as the man got to the top. Then at last the TV chatter stopped as his apartment door closed.

Maja came back around midnight. Alice had made another pot of fennel tea, with honey, drinking it all, along with three of the child's biscuits. She had pulled open several kitchen drawers, had gazed at the contents and closed them again. In the cutlery drawer, countless little spoons rattling around, spoons from cough-medicine packages, tiny ice-cream spoons, plastic spoons. Messy, she said under her breath. Below the video recorder there were cassettes with handwritten labels, dubious content. On the recessed shelves, art paper, scissors, and used-up glue sticks. It was getting more and more depressing. She forced herself to stop looking.

She'd emptied the dishwasher, putting the plates and cups into the cupboard above the stove, an involuntary imitation of a different life. Had tried to resist watching TV, then capitulated. She had fallen asleep at the table, head on her arms, safe in the random order of the objects around her: teats, Maja's barrette, tea bags, crayons, and a children's cardboard book with soft corners. Suddenly she started up, her hands were numb. But the child was still sound asleep, her left hand tightly clamped around the rabbit's ear, and no heavy shadow in the hall outside the door. Alice went into the room where she would be sleeping, had opened the couch and made up her bed. A blue sheet. Her nightgown next to the pillow. Shades down, patio door open. A gentle breeze outside, the brave constancy of things, their unambiguous names, the child would learn them all: tree, chair, garden, sky, moon, and hospital. Lit-up windows, dark windows. Small figures behind them, a Maja, a Misha, a nun.

11:45 PM.

Night watch.

Maja came back silently, without making a sound on the stairs or in the hallway; there was only her knock on the frosted glass pane. She was surprised to find that Alice had locked the door, Was everything all right? Yes, Alice said, everything's all right, but it made me feel better this way.

Maja went to check on the child, briefly and conscientiously; she always seemed to have just enough strength for the things that had to be considered or done, no more and no less, precise and appropriate. Alice, sitting at the table, waited, her back erect, hands folded in her lap.

Want a beer? Maja asked.

Sure.

For a long time Alice rummaged among the plastic spoons for an opener, finally found one with the name of a service area near Bad Zwischenahn on it, took two bottles of beer out of the refrigerator, ice-cold. They clinked bottles, without saying a word. The beer tingled, tasting sweet; slowly it toned down something inside Alice's head and made it go away. Expanding, stretching inwardly with alcohol? She'd read that somewhere; it seemed to be true.

It was nice at the hospital, Maja said. Very peaceful. They let me lie down next to Misha. We lay together like that for the first time in a long time. He was breathing quietly. I don't think he was in pain. Tomorrow, around noon, I can talk with the doctor after he's been to see Misha. Could be I even fell asleep for a little while. We slept together.

When did you first meet actually? Alice asked casually.

Don't you know? Maja said. Pleasantly. Amazed.

No, Alice said. She really didn't know. Misha had never mentioned it, but then she had never asked him.

The day you came back from the trip you took together.

Oh. Really? Alice said, astonished. That trip had been years ago; it was the only trip she'd ever taken with Misha, and at the end of it they had agreed to separate. I'm breaking it off now, Misha had said, once and for all. And Alice had answered, confidently, Yes, me too. They'd been content together, didn't argue, maybe that's why they were able to break it off. Misha had left first. Alice had stayed on a few more days. She suddenly remembered how she had started to cry after she'd taken him to the station and was driving back to the house by herself. As if he had died – she thought, Well, I've gone through that. I have it behind me.

Maja said, Misha was happy when he came back. When I first met him. He was doing well, he was fairly well rested.

It was the sea air, Alice said. The change in climate.

They said nothing for a while. Alice hesitated, then she said, The last evening of our trip we were sitting together – just like you and me now. Together at a table, with two bottles of beer, only it was in a garden, and it was June – but you know that already. The millennium-summer June. Still very hot, even in the middle of the night.

She thought about it, how suggestive that sounded – hot, middle of the night, millennium-summer June. Together, you and me. How vivid, the words behind the words. But that's how it had been, one evening before Misha met Maja; who would have thought.

And then? Maja asked.

And then a spider began to spin a web between our two beer bottles, Alice said. The first threads between the bottle-necks. She indicated the size of the spider with her thumb and index finger, a grain of rice. The fine, thin strand strung between the two bottles as if over an abyss. They had been sitting next to each other, shoulder to shoulder. Watching the little spider for a while, weaving so serenely, so self-absorbed.

He was sorry, Alice said. He was sorry that he'd have to destroy her work.

And did he destroy it? Maja asked.

Well, take a guess, Alice said. They both laughed, each one softly to herself.

C'mon, let's go to bed, Maja said. It's already half past one. We have to get up early tomorrow. Do you want to go and see him in the morning?

And Alice said, Yes, I'd like to see him again in the morning.

They brushed their teeth. Standing next to each other at the sink on a blue towelling mat, in front of a mirror that had gold and silver shells glued to its frame. They saw each other in the mirror, their different faces.

Misha would like this, Alice thought, to see us like this. He'd be very happy, he'd say, Well, you see? – He knows. He's got to know.

Good night, Alice said. Sleep well, Maja.

Yes, Maja said, good night. You sleep well, too, Alice.

Alice woke up when Maja knocked on her bedroom door, calling her name. Maybe she'd been knocking for quite a while already. Alice was having a hard time emerging from a deep, exhausted sleep. Later she wondered why Maja hadn't simply come into the room. Then she was awake. A momentary memory of her childhood and what it was like to be roused in the middle of the night to go on summer holiday. Terror and excitement. She threw back the covers and called out, I'm awake. Maja opened the door and stood there with the child on her arm, a cut-out, silhouetted against the bright living room where the lamp above the table was on again, and she said, Misha is dead.

How late is it? Alice asked.

Four o'clock, Maja said. The hospital called. He died two hours ago; they just wanted to let us sleep a little longer.

Wait. I'll get up, Alice said. She put a sweater over her nightgown, then walked barefoot into the kitchen. The child was sitting at the table, thumb in mouth, without her sleeping bag, wearing a little blue shirt with snap fasteners on the shoulder. Petit Bateau. Alice rubbed her eyes. Maja was just standing there in the middle of the room. Astronauts, Alice thought, we're like astronauts, there's no place to hold on to.

They wanted to know whether we'd like to see him once more, Maja said. If so, they'd wait for us. She looked utterly frightened by that.

I have to think about it, Alice said; it sounded like a question. She sat down next to the child, propped her elbows on the table. Just a moment. I have to think.

Have you ever seen a dead person?

No. I haven't.

Maja called the hospital and said, We're coming. Could they please wait, we need a little time because of the child and the time it takes to get there, maybe half an hour, would that be possible.

Who was on the phone? Alice asked.

Don't know, one of the nuns, Maja said. Not the old, severe one; a young nun.

All right then, Alice said. Let's go.

That afternoon she left for Berlin.

Maja might have stayed, but Alice felt she'd go crazy if she had to spend one more night in that apartment with the view of the hospital in which no one was lying any more. The hospital was hollow, empty. A silent shell.

If we're not careful, Alice thought, we'll disappear too, Maja, the child, and I; we'll vanish without a trace in Zweibrücken.

She phoned the railway station and they gave her an exhausting train connection; she wrote the times down in her diary, a magic formula, something to hold on to. Maja and the child would fly back that evening. Together they tidied the apartment, stripped the beds, rinsed the cups, and packed their things, while the child played on the floor in front of the TV, building towers with the plastic blocks and destroying them again, building and destroying, until she lost control.

Come, let's go back to sleep, Maja said to the child, lying down on the bed with her and breaking into tears. Alice carefully closed the door. She sat down at the table and drank three large mugs of cold, bitter, black coffee, one right after the other. In the garden on the hillside that sloped down to the valley the man was sawing some cheap wood; he didn't look up to the terrace. He hadn't given Alice another glance, hadn't said a single word to her, everything had already been said. But he embraced Maja when she paid for the night and had to tell him and his wife what had happened. Maja took no notice of the embrace. No damage done. Alice had watched in amazement; Maja was a widow, vulnerable and sacred, she didn't have to be asked whether she had everything she needed, and her answer would surely have been different from Alice's. The wife had stuffed the rental money into the pocket of her cardigan, pretending she wasn't going to count it, and then as if on cue, had begun to lament, raising her hands to heaven. Alice had gone into the bathroom and waited there till it was over.

I'll drive you to the airport, the woman said to Maja. Of course I will. I'll drive you to the airport this evening; and Alice had said she'd take a taxi to the train station even though no one had asked her.

Maja and the child slept for two more hours. Then they got up, each in her own way sleepy and confused. The child's bare feet on the kitchen floor made a sound that Alice couldn't stand. She said, I have to go now. She had to restrain herself to keep from putting on her jacket then and there.

I know, Maja said. It's all right; I still have some things to do here, and then in a little while we'll be driving to the airport. Would you take Misha's suitcase with you? I'll pick it up later at your place in Berlin.

It was a small suitcase. With wheels, not heavy. At the hospital that afternoon when the room had to be cleared, Maja had sorted Misha's things. Sunlight was falling on the shiny linoleum and on the plastic sheet covering the freshly made bed. The nurses had given them a bin bag. Alice held the bag open and Maja lifted up each item in turn: pills, information about alternative cancer treatments, new socks, new pyjamas, slippers – all went into the bin bag. The things Misha had worn when he was flown to Zweibrücken went into the suitcase; the photo of Maja and the child, into the suitcase; the notebook with the blank pages, into the suitcase. They took the bag back to the nurses' station. The child was sitting in the lap of one of the nuns and was saying newly learned words to herself, repeating them over and over, proudly, but hard to understand. Actually it sounded like: Abra. Ca. Dabra:

Abracadabra. It really did.

I don't mind taking the suitcase, Alice said. I'm grateful to you. I don't mind at all. She had no words for what she really wanted to say.

The cab driver was walking up the garden path. On the broken paving stones, past the flower beds and the clay turtle. The taxi was black, a limousine with tinted windows, no name of a cab company visible.

But this is a taxi, isn't it? Alice said, not at all sure; everything was out of sync, anything was possible. The cab driver didn't deign to answer the question. He took the suitcase from Alice, her overnight bag, retraced his steps, and loaded everything into the boot; then he got in, waiting.

We'll see each other in Berlin, Alice said.

Yes, Maja said. She was standing in the open doorway with the child on her arm. The straw witch rustled in the draft. The azaleas in the conservatory. Afternoon light. Have a good trip.

Alice turned and walked through the garden, out to the street, and to the cab. She got into the back, rolled down the window and waved. Maja waved back. She said something to the child, the child waved too. The cab started up. Maja stepped inside the front hall with the child, closing the door behind her.

II

Conrad

They had directions for getting there. Conrad had sent them to Alice in Berlin the old-fashioned way, by mail: the address, telephone number, and a little sketch of the house in which he and Lotte lived, a white rectangle, and the yellow house south of it. Conrad's handwriting was delicate and shaky, already familiar to her. How quickly you can get to know someone's handwriting, Alice thought, much more quickly than the person himself. The sketch was in her lap. She was wearing a crumpled, flowered skirt and sitting in the passenger seat. Anna was sleeping in the back, her head leaning against her backpack, her arm over her face. The Romanian was driving. Ever since they had crossed the border into Italy, he had been speaking Italian.

Seemed to have become another person. He asked, Know what the word for cream is in Italian? Alice said she didn't know. Why of all things, cream? Incomprehensible.

And the other way round – from Italian into German – *macchiato*? *Latte macchiato*?

I don't know, Alice said Aren't you listening to me? I don't know it the other way round either.

Stained milk, the Romanian said. Stained milk.

They took the Rovereto Sud exit. Continuing in the direction of Riva, still thirty kilometres to Gargnano Bogliaco. Then the mountains opened up to a view of the lake. Glorious. Dark blue. Countless white sails, a flotilla. It got hotter and yet at the same time cooler – all you had to do was look at the water. The water is ice cold; it's a mountain lake, after all, said the Romanian who had been here before.

Frosta or something, Alice said irritably.

Something like that, the Romanian said, smiling to himself. He'd also been holding the wheel differently since they'd crossed the border, more relaxed, with just his left hand, steering with just his left hand into a tunnel. Its blackness took her breath away until she realised that she ought to take off her sunglasses. Anna, in the back seat, woke up. They were gliding out of the tunnel again – cypresses to the right, the lake to the left, blinding light and very sharp turns, then another tunnel. Can you sense your pupils contracting, Alice said to Anna, turning round, and she felt how sweaty she was.

This is crazy, Anna said. We've got to stop, right now. I feel really sick.

They stopped after a bend in the road. Anna and Alice stood next to each other beside a stone parapet and looked out over the water, so misty in the distance, you couldn't see the other shore. Palm trees. Lemon trees. The mountains, dark and gloomy. There was nothing but the mountains, then the road, then the water. Actually no landscape, little space for people, cramped and spacious at the same time.

Do you think this is beautiful? Anna asked.

I don't know, Alice said. It probably is very beautiful. Isn't it?

The Romanian, standing somewhere behind them clicked the shutter of his camera. They could hear it. A panoramic view: Anna and Alice at the lake.

OK, Alice said, you have to keep your eyes open now. I think we'll be there soon. *Attenzione, capito?*

Five o'clock in the afternoon on the road between Gargnano Bogliaco and Toscolano-Maderno. Seen from above, a little car on the road that runs along the shore of the lake – Anna in the back, the Romanian and Alice in the front, baggage in the boot, water bottles rolling around on the floor and ashtrays full of cigarette butts, paper ice-cream wrappers and foil from packs of cigarettes. The excitement now infects all three, the car windows are open, Anna holding her hand out of the window into the air rushing by, and Alice calls out: Turn right! Here. Bear right, up there on the right towards that restaurant, keep to the right, go past it. Right, exactly. We're almost there.

Fifty metres from here, Conrad had written, there's a spot where five roads come together. Take the one that leads through the forged-iron gate, the 'fifth road'. It leads to the yellow house.

The fifth road is a dirt road. To the left a little stream, an olive grove, and among the trees, goats raising their heads, indifferent. The car rocks from side to side. They pass Lotte and Conrad's house, a large, old, converted barn in the bend of the road on the side of the mountain, tall windows facing the lake, shutters closed tight. Ahead, at the end of the road, the yellow house. An Italian palazzo. Shuttered up, ivy, two balconies, one facing the mountain, the other the lake. A terrace, fig trees, agaves, and bougainvillea. From the back seat Anna says, You can actually hear the cicadas. There is rapt amazement in her voice. They get out of the car, leaving the doors open and going off in different directions.

Alice walked up the dirt road to Conrad and Lotte's house. Pebbles in her sandals. She looked up at the black mountain behind the house and ducked. She climbed the broad steps between huge, tropical lavender bushes. Cardinal beetles, bright red, their little bodies chained to each other. In a hurry. And a rustling in the trees, a light breeze. Lotte was sitting on the terrace, which was empty except for a green hose on a drum, a grey stone sphere and the chair in which she sat. Three doors on the lower part of the house, two of them closed, the middle one slightly ajar. Lotte got up as Alice reached the terrace and came towards her; they greeted each other with a tentative embrace, cautiously, as if, at a touch, the other might dissolve into thin air.

There you are, Lotte said. She smiled and then stopped smiling. When she wasn't smiling the creases around her eyes were white. Lotte was seventy years old. Conrad too. More than twenty-five years older than Alice. Did everything go all right. Lotte said. Did you have a good trip. She asked the questions so that they sounded like statements but still she expected an answer.

Yes, Alice said. Everything went well. It was strenuous, but now we're here, and we're happy to be here. Lotte, I'm so very happy.

Lotte said, Conrad is sick. Unfortunately he's sick, nothing serious, only a little fever, but he's in bed.

She indicated the middle door; it was dark behind the door, not a sound to be heard.

He doesn't want you to see him lying in bed; he doesn't want that. He'll come to see you later, Lotte smiled again, a smile somewhere between irony and sadness. She was tanned from the Italian sun, wore a lightweight linen dress, unwrinkled, pale violet, falling in precise folds, and a necklace of silvery, smooth beads. She looked neat and rested; Alice thought of all the motorway rest stops of the past ten hours, of the radio music in the toilets, the smell of urine and disinfectant, the broken soap dispensers, of her own exhausted face reflected in a mirror of scratched tin. She was glad she didn't have to say hello to Conrad just now; he would be able to retain his image of her arrival: a picture of an arrival.

Come, said Lotte softly. I'll unlock the yellow house for you.

She held up two small keys that she had probably been holding in her hand all the while. She had been sitting on the terrace, holding the keys, waiting for them. And, Alice thought, it was really Conrad who had invited them. It had been his invitation; of course he must have discussed the invitation with Lotte, but it had been his idea. Come and visit us and bring along whomever you like. Alice decided to ask Anna, she didn't want to go anywhere without Anna. And she picked the Romanian because he was always polite and knew how to behave. Maybe also because she wasn't in love with him. As far as she knew, Anna wasn't in love with him either. She had suggested their names to Conrad, and he had agreed. And now he was sick. A fever. He would have unlocked the yellow house and shown it to them. Alice knew he would have enjoyed that very much. She followed Lotte down the stairs, Lotte's slow, measured steps, not turning to look again at the middle door. The cardinal beetles scurried out of their way and vanished into the cracks between the stones.

The yellow house had three storeys and six rooms. Alice chose the room under the eaves, the room Conrad used to live in, before he and Lotte converted *la stalla*. The room was square, windows on two sides, a narrow bed, a cupboard, a red carpet with a black pattern woven into it and, in its exact centre, a table. From there Alice could see the peaks of the mountains on the other side of the lake. Anna took the room next door. Fig leaves on the coverlet over the wide bed, a door leading to the second balcony and another to a bathroom with a bathtub, shiny fixtures, blue tiles, and two sinks in front of two mirrors. A stairway led down to the first floor, no banister, instead a golden cord along the wall which slid softly through Alice's hand. The sheets, starched and ironed, were in a chest under the stairway. The Romanian took the smallest room for himself. Its window was shaded by ivy; it had a metal bed with a small table next to it, polished wood, delicate inlaid work. On the ground floor: the kitchen, a dining room, a living room, low sofas in front of the fireplace and on the bookshelf were games for rainy days: Monopoly, Ludo, chess. On the walls hung framed drawings by their children, Lotte and Conrad's children, three. And drawings by the grandchildren, five. A guest book next to the telephone. In the large pantry behind the kitchen was a refrigerator into which Conrad had put a watermelon the day before. Alice went from room to room pushing open all the shutters, then the doors to the balconies; the curtain rings clattered softly against each other. Sunlight on the table in Conrad's old room, and fine dust.

Anna opened her backpack, threw everything on the bed: white skirts, dresses, and blouses with red roses on them. Suntan lotion. Books. Three pairs of sunglasses. From downstairs the Romanian called up to them: Campari! It was really quite unbearable.

Leaning against the door frame of Anna's room, her naked feet crossed and her arms across her chest, Alice asked, Do you suppose we'll still be going for a swim today?

Well, *naturalmente*, Anna said, what do you think!

One of the kitchen doors led to the outside, the other into the dining room. Seventeen steps from the kitchen to the dining room, living room, and a white French door to the terrace. The terrace was the seventh room; it had a stone parapet with red cushions on it, three columns, a cypress. Alice sat down on the bench outside the house next to the kitchen door. Lizards on the house wall, their mysterious rustling in the ivy. No breeze now. Nothing. She sat there like that for a while. Then she got up and went into the kitchen, walked past the Romanian without saying a word, and the seventeen steps again to the terrace where Anna was sitting on the stone parapet on the red cushions, leaning against a column, holding a glass in her left hand, her knees drawn up, her head to one side, and her matted hair tied into a child's pigtail. She smiled at Alice, showing her broken left front tooth. What a relief to see her.

What a relief to see you, Alice said. You have no idea, you just wouldn't believe it.

And what if I do? Anna said.

That doesn't change anything, Alice said.

After the sun had set, they walked along the dirt road, past the goats, through the great forged-iron gate, and down to the restaurant on the lakeshore road. Nuovo Ponte, it was called. Lotte had said they should have supper there, drink a glass of wine, and leave the shopping until tomorrow. She asked Alice to introduce Anna and the Romanian to her, but seemed absent-minded and rather apathetic, giving them only a quick and knowing glance. She had apologised for Conrad's indisposition and had postponed their celebratory meal together until the following day. The Romanian had been exceptionally obliging and charming, Anna had been, too; she just wasn't able to hide her preference for leaving all this, to desert so she could be on her own. Lotte had taken note of this, casually but accurately. She also took note of the pigtail. The broken tooth. The neckline of Anna's dress, and what all these things said about Alice. All three of them had revealed themselves.

They walked peaceably next to each other. The Romanian in the middle, Anna on his left, Alice on his right. And you'll order for us, Alice said. You're going to take care of all that. Wine and olives and sardines and bread. And tomorrow you'll go to the barber. And have your hair cut. By a barbiere. Alice felt her head would burst if she couldn't immediately have a glass of wine to drink. The Romanian handled everything with ease. Playfully. Ironically. He picked a table near the street, a round table with a white tablecloth, set under a lemon tree on the pebble strip in the small garden in front of the *ristorante*. He greeted the waiters and answered their stock phrases, *buon giorno, come va, bene, grazie, bene, grazie, benissimo*; he flipped open the menus and closed them, recapitulated the vineyards, vintages, grape varieties. Alice closed her eyes. Then drank the red wine. They ate sardines and peppers and little slices of white bread soaked in olive oil. The Romanian talked about his childhood summer holidays. Weeks spent on the eastern shore of the lake, on the opposite side, at a campground. They had stayed in a caravan with a tent and plastic chairs, waking every morning, getting up, and heading straight for the lake, swimming far out. Thunder, the gathering and passing of thunderstorms. Black mould on the walls of the caravan, like filigree blossoms. Rubber boots, rain jackets, and instead of sweets, sucking grainy Instant Tea powder till your tongue was thick and bloated. Suntan oil. Algae on the water. Fog. Once they had gone up the mountain in the cable car, actually finding snow on top, a lunar landscape, grey rocks and the air very thin; then, back down in the cable car, into the insane certainty of the heat. In the evening, playing canasta with cards swollen from the humidity. Rummy. Bridge. Clammy sleeping bags. Mosquitoes swarming around the camping lantern and the smell of paraffin, the smoking wick.

And I still remember what it was like, the Romanian said. It's long ago, but I remember exactly what it was like. Alice thought that the Romanian was a happy man in Italy. She didn't know why, but it was easy to see. He went into raptures. His ears stuck out; his face glowed.

It's just the way of life here, Anna said, shrugging; she raised her glass of wine and said, *Salute*, and, Look, there's Lotte. She pointed to the street, where Lotte was just getting out of her car in the orange light of the street lamp.

Alice pushed her chair back and got up, but remained standing by the table until Lotte reached them. In the crunching of the pebbles and the sound of the other diners' voices there was a lane of silence, through which Lotte walked towards their table. Lotte gestured with her left hand for them to stay, Don't get up, please. It's nothing, she said, but Conrad is feeling somewhat worse; we're driving to the hospital. They'll probably send us home again. Still, I feel better going there. His fever is very high ... What did you have to eat? Aha, sardines. The sardines are very good at the Nuovo Ponte. But next time you have to order squid, grilled.

Can I talk to Conrad, just briefly? Alice asked.

Of course, Lotte said.

Conrad was sitting in the front seat, the seat back had been lowered to a reclining position; he was lying rather than sitting, but he wore a neatly pressed, elegant, light-coloured shirt and smiled mockingly at Alice's worried expression. She opened the car door and they shook hands. He held her hand in both of his. His hands were dry and hot. Dear Alice. He said, We didn't imagine it would be like this, did we? Seeing each other again, I mean. But that's just the way it is, and tomorrow things will be better. It's such an odd coincidence. Perhaps I got too excited about your arrival.

Alice said nothing. She let her hand remain in his. He looked past her towards the table where the Romanian and Anna were sitting, and said, So there they are, the friends I don't know. He squinted slightly. Dark Anna and the Romanian. We'll say hello tomorrow. Are you all right?

Yes, Alice said, her voice serious. All drunkenness, exhausted nervousness, and irritation were suddenly gone. We're doing fine, Conrad. I only wish you were feeling better.

I am feeling better, Conrad said. The admissions people at the hospital will send me right back home again. Lotte's worried, that's all.

Lotte got into the car, closed the door, pulled the seat belt over her shoulder and turned the key in the ignition. A transparent rock hung down from the key chain, shaped like a large teardrop. Conrad let go of Alice's hand.

All right, then, see you soon.

Yes, see you soon, Alice said. She straightened up, closed the car door as gently as possible and watched the car as it rolled down the street, turned into the lakeshore road, and was gone.

Lotte came back in the middle of the night. Half past one. Or half past two? They couldn't remember precisely. They had been at the Nuovo Ponte till closing time. What Lotte hadn't known was that none of them would be able to stop at just one glass of wine. The usual drinking rituals – just one more goodnight grappa before leaving, and another, and then one last one. They took two bottles of wine along with them, paying a whopper of a bill. And then back through the forged-iron gate along the dirt road, past the dark house on the side of the hill and towards the yellow house where they had left the lights on and the doors open. There it was, waiting for them, enchanted and silent. Which spot was really the most beautiful? The bench outside the kitchen. The balcony facing the lake with the trembling lights on the far shore, the Romanian's camping site, the paraffin lamps of his childhood. Or Anna's balcony, the compact opacity of the mountain, a black massif against the night sky. The three of them were completely drunk. They sat down on the terrace – it was the best spot, this seventh room with its stone parapet, three columns and the cypress, sharp-edged and closed, like a feather.

They opened a bottle of wine, which took a while. The Romanian couldn't deal with the corkscrew, but by now Alice's impatience had diminished, throbbing only a little now and then as if to itself. They sat together in a triangle, the bottle, glasses, and a carafe of water between them, a saucer as ashtray; the candle flickered in the draught, and fat fireflies darted about in the meadow down below. They talked about this and that, nothing important. Telling each other stories. Alice said something to Anna, and Anna replied while the Romanian listened; they were gentle with one another, exhausted and gentle.

Lotte might have been standing on the two steps that led from the terrace into the garden for quite a while before they saw her. At some point she said something and came over to sit with them on the edge of the parapet. She said they had kept Conrad in the hospital after all; the fever had been too high for too long. No cause for concern, only a routine evaluation of test results tomorrow morning during the first doctors' rounds. She said she'd like to be there for that, to talk to the doctors, shortly after seven o'clock; would it be possible for one of them to drive her to the hospital? She was very tired, not able to concentrate on the road.

Of course, said the Romanian. Of course I'll drive you to the hospital. He was so drunk that he almost babbled, but it didn't matter; despite that he was reacting well, appropriately, confidently.

All right, then, Lotte said. I'm sorry. Till tomorrow. We should leave at six fifteen.

She got up. Alice thought she was very tall, an erect, straight figure. Severe-looking but forbearing. Loyal.

Good, said the Romanian, he got up too. Till tomorrow, then, at a quarter past six.

Lotte left. She disappeared as soundlessly as she had come, having turned down their offer to accompany her to the house on the hill, those hundred steps on the dirt road and then up through the lavender. No, thanks.

What time is it, Alice asked. How late is it? You're completely drunk; how are you going to drive the car tomorrow at six fifteen? How's that supposed to work?

Well, should I not drive her? the Romanian said coolly.

Yes, yes, you should, Alice said. She was panicky, wide awake. Did Lotte really know. Just now, did she realise what's going on here, how completely drunk we are.

The Romanian giggled.

She did, Anna said. Of course she realised it; you couldn't miss it. But so what? We'll all go; we'll set three alarm clocks. It'll work out. We'll manage. Calm down, Alice.

You're the one least likely to wake up when the alarm goes off, Alice said. Well, good night, I have to go to sleep right now.

Alice went upstairs. Concentrating hard. Keep your wits about you, she thought, pull yourself together. She thought:

Conrad. She climbed the stairs to the first floor, to the second. She washed at the left sink. Leaving the light on over the mirror for Anna, she walked through Anna's room into her room, Conrad's room. She opened the window, closed the curtains, and pulled her dress off over her head. She set the travel alarm clock for five thirty, and didn't count the hours till then. She got into bed, closed her eyes. She could hear the voice of the Romanian downstairs, then Anna's voice, both low and mysterious.

Dog days, the Romanian said. Look up there. Pegasus and Andromeda. Cassiopeia and Cepheus. And the Big Dragon keeps moving around the sky and never sleeps. If we're lucky, we'll be able to see Jupiter.

How does that old saying go? Anna said.

Which saying?

Oh, the saying we used to remember the planets by when we were kids. You never heard of it? – My very enthusiastic mother just served ... and so forth and so on.

My very enthusiastic mother just served us noodle pudding, the Romanian said. His voice so calm, Anna's voice too, they were saying it together now: Mercury, Venus, Earth, Mars, Jupiter, Saturn, Uranus, Neptune, and Pluto.

Have we got them all? Anna asked.

It all depends, the Romanian said.

Whatever, Anna said, and Alice knew exactly the kind of face she was making, an expression of contentment and warmth on her round face. Saturn is in my seventh house.

In the sign of the zodiac, do you know what I mean? The seventh house is the house of doors. Through which people come to you and leave you. The planets move slowly but they make their transits, and then your whole life changes, it changes whether you want it to or not. Now Saturn is coming. He moves in opposition to Uranus. And everything, everything will be different.

She laughed, the Romanian didn't. Alice turned over on her side, stopped listening. One moment more. Then she was out of it.

Dawn came at half past five in the morning. The Romanian was standing at the stove in the kitchen, turning down the gas as the coffee began to rise, hissing, in the espresso maker. He had heated some milk in a little pot with a wooden handle. He poured the coffee into two round white cups, remembering that Alice drank hers with milk and no sugar, adding the milk, the foam at the end. Had he slept? He looked awake and rested. Handing Alice her cup, he made a noise that sounded vaguely like the mewing of a very small kitten. Alice was at a loss. They sat down next to each other on the bench outside the kitchen door. The sky over the mountain turned blue. A light was on in Lotte's house. Ice-cold bird voices and the smell of lavender. The Romanian was listening to something, then he said, Did you know that birds with the largest eyes sing earliest in the morning?

No, I didn't know. Sounds odd.

The Romanian nodded. Sounds odd, yes. But that's the way it is. The more light, the more singing.

Alice blew on her coffee. She cleared her throat and said, What's Anna doing?

Still sleeping, the Romanian said. I think you ought to wake her up, better do it with a wet flannel.

I'd do it if I knew where she was, Alice said irritably.

In my room, the Romanian said.

How come? Alice said.

Yes, I'd like to know that too, the Romanian said. He apparently found it highly amusing. She seemed to think we'd have an easier time being awakened by the alarm clock if we were together.

You wake her up, Alice said. I don't feel like it.

The Romanian said nothing. He drank his coffee in delicate sips, calmly sitting on the bench, one leg crossed over the other. When he got up he briefly, lightly touched Alice's hand.

They drove into town in Lotte's car. A white BMW, air-conditioned, with tinted windows. The Romanian drove, Lotte sat next to him, Anna and Alice slumped in the back seat, both wearing sunglasses. The landscape slipped by noiselessly, lakeshore, pebble beaches, classicist villas, pilgrimage churches, greenhouses up and down the hillsides. Lotte and the Romanian were talking about growing lemons. Thirteenth-century. Franciscan monks. *Zardi de limú*, the Romanian said, cheerful and polite, and then Lotte's voice, refined, very cultivated, subtly and gently pointing at the hillsides.

Limonaie.

Or *Limonare*?

The Romanian wasn't sure either; he said, Up there, see those masonry posts they used to put wood and glass panes on top of them in the wintertime – protection for the lemon trees against the cold. Today they're just ruins, he was saying this to Anna and Alice, looking at them in the rear-view mirror. Alice returned his look and knew that he couldn't tell she was doing so because of her sunglasses. She wished he would look into the rear-view mirror once more, would look into it again a little later without saying anything about masonry posts. A silent look. But he didn't.

There were boats on the lake, probably red ones, and bougainvillea growing over the balconies of the houses, probably purple; the tinted windows swallowed all colour. Nobody said anything about Conrad. Lotte didn't ask how they had slept. Alice couldn't have answered the question. She hadn't slept. She was out and then she was back again as though someone had hit her over the head. She looked at Anna and knew it was the same with her, and she had to laugh. Holding up her hand, Anna tried to get Alice to stop laughing, then put the hand to her forehead, indicating she had a terrible headache. We'll get some Coca-Cola, Alice said softly. Soon. They left the lakeshore road, drove through an intersection, mundane traffic lights, suddenly everything actually did seem to be grey. Lotte gave directions matter-of-factly. A large parking area in front of the hospital. Lotte opened the car door; the sky was white. Go swimming, Lotte said. Come back at noon to pick me up. Straight-backed, her head held high, an elegant but empty-looking braided bag over her left shoulder, she walked across the car park, past a little gatehouse, a closed barricade. She looked like a young girl. Didn't look back. The Romanian turned the car round.

The lake was ice cold. The water clear as glass. When Alice dived in, it took her breath away, an incomprehensible, ecstatic suffocation. Everything was different. Everything was perfect. She extended her entire body underwater, a long stretching from her fingertips to her toes, then she spread her arms and swam. She swam submerged for a long time, and when she came up again she was far away from the shore. Turning, she saw the dock above the choppy surface of the water, behind it a wall of red stone, a gate in the wall, cedars behind the gate, then the mountain. On the dock, a very small Anna. In a blue bikini. Lying on a towel. Next to a bright yellow bottle of suntan lotion. To her right and left, the deserted white pebble beach.

How am I going to tell her what it looks like? Alice thought. How can I show her, how can she know how beautiful it is?

She raised her hand and waved while treading water, spat, out of breath. Anna waved back, calling out something incomprehensible. The Romanian was even further out than Alice; actually she couldn't see him now, his little head. Short, choppy waves on the lake. It was as deep as the mountains surrounding it were high. Alice turned and swam back.

What's the difference between a cicada and a cricket?

Is that supposed to be a joke?

No, I'm serious. I don't know the difference. But there must be one. I once had a wooden box with a cricket made of metal inside. It made a cricket noise when you raised the cover. Something to do with the light. The light making the metal vibrate? From a Vietnamese. From the Vietnamese market.

Aha, Anna said. She yawned, and turned from her back onto her stomach. She gazed out over the water, cupping a hand above her eyes. I think cicadas are big and crickets are small. Are cicadas green and crickets grey? Do only the females chirp? What's the name of the mountain on the far side of the lake? I think I've got to go into the water again, right now. I can't stand it. Everything's hot here. The pebbles. Even the suntan lotion is hot. Stop smoking, Alice, it's unbearable.

Monte Baldo, the Romanian said. The mountain is Monte Baldo. In our country it's called a head cricket, it crawls into your skull and causes insanity and death. We're surrounded by them. Cedars and crickets wherever you look. If you want to go in again, you ought to do it now. Right now. We have to get back. It's almost noon.

Anna repeated his words, disparagingly. A head cricket. She grimaced in disgust, pursed her lips. Alice fished for her sunglasses with her toes, put them on and looked at the Romanian. His narrow shoulders, hips, ankles, feet. Everything. He had held out the suntan lotion to Alice and Anna; it was a question. Alice had turned away; Anna had rubbed the lotion on the Romanian's slender back. The Romanian hadn't met Conrad yet. Neither had Anna. They didn't share her worries. But the Romanian was very attentive, and Alice was grateful for that. She got up, slipped skirt and blouse on over her bathing suit, picked up her sandals with her left hand, climbed down from the dock, and walked back across the pebble beach to the street. She felt weak. The pebbles were glowing hot, and every step hurt.

At the hospital Lotte was sitting right in the middle of a long bench in front of the lifts, her bag in her lap, and facing a panoramic window with a view of the car park. The lift disgorged Anna, Alice, and the Romanian with a plucking, mechanical sound. Lotte was smiling as if she were asleep; she didn't get up, scarcely moved at all. Alice looked at the clock above the lift doors – a little after twelve. Is that what Lotte meant when she said they should come around noon? Simple arrangements, made just once, had something confusing about them. Lotte was used to making decisions, Alice could sense that. A decision maker. She looked more rested than she had that morning, more calm. Now she turned to Alice; Anna and the Romanian deferentially took a step back.

He's doing much better, Lotte said. The fever has gone down; he'll come home soon; but they want to keep him another night to be on the safe side. An infection? She raised her eyebrows and thought about the word; it seemed to be the right one. They suspect it's an infection. That happens sometimes here; after all, the climate is almost tropical. She gave a dry laugh, then she got up. Well, he wants to see you now. It's the room at the end of the corridor.

She pointed down the long corridor; it was glistening, bright. It seemed like more than one could handle. Did you go swimming?

Don't you want to come along? Alice asked, her heart pounding in her throat.

No, Lotte said. I was with him all morning. Go on. Go by yourself.

Alice started down the corridor. She heard the Romanian taking up the thread of the conversation – Yes, we went swimming. Down at that little bathing spot, a private beach? Very romantic. A little dock. In front of the red wall with the gate leading to a neglected garden.

Conrad was lying in bed, near the window. A green, half-drawn venetian blind; the room filled with rulers of light. No air conditioner, only a ceiling fan. Come, sit next to me, Conrad said. He lightly patted the bed. Alice sat down on the edge of the bed. Conrad was naked, a white, thin sheet covering his loins, that was all. Alice, seeing him naked for the first time, was amazed how beautiful he was, an old, naked man with white chest hair and brown skin, a little lighter in the soft bends of the arms and at the neck; he looked solid; there was nothing fragile about him. She thought, If he weren't sick, I would have seen him like this for the first time when we went swimming, and she didn't know which she would have preferred: Would it have been his nakedness in this bed? Perhaps.

Conrad's breathing was shallow; he gazed steadily at Alice, searchingly, proud. He said, What a lot of nonsense. What nonsense that I should be lying here and just when you've come. It's high time for all this to stop. I'm going home tomorrow. It's unbearable this way. You know I want to see you in the water, you have to go swimming with me, did you go swimming today?

Yes, Alice said. Truthfully and obediently. We went swimming. Near your place, down at the beach near the villa.

Was it cold?

Yes, it was cold.

Conrad nodded; it seemed to be very important to him that the water was cold. Alice thought it important too.

And which room are you sleeping in?

In your room, Alice said. She added, Anna is sleeping in the room next to it. The Romanian in the little room near the stairs. She was sure that Conrad would be enchanted by Anna. By the lightness below her dark side. Platonic affection, tendernesses – like those for people in books, imagined feelings.

Well, Conrad said. You should drive to Salò today, and have a drink on the lake promenade, that red stuff. Lotte will tell you what it's called; it's what everybody drinks here in the afternoon. With ice and lemon. You do that. I'll be home tomorrow.

All right, Alice said.

She didn't know what else to say, but she didn't want to get up either. She wondered if Conrad might still have a bit of fever; heat seemed to be rising from his brown skin, but maybe it was only the heat in the room. Midday heat, the tropical climate. Conrad raised his hand and touched Alice's face. He had never done that before. He put the back of his hand briefly on Alice's cheek, pinched it slightly as if she were a child. He said thoughtfully, You know, I thought I was invulnerable. That's what I thought.

He shook his head and looked towards the window, towards the light between the green slats of the blind; then he looked again at Alice and said, All right, then, till tomorrow. Drive carefully.

Till tomorrow, Alice said. She got up, stood by the bed, raised her shoulders and lowered them again. They both smiled. Alice left the room, went down the long, brightly lit hallway back to the lift. They were now sitting next to one another, Lotte in the middle between Anna and the Romanian, and Alice stopped in front of them. The Romanian looked out at the car park. Anna looked at Lotte. No one said anything.

He's feeling better, isn't he? Lotte said.

I think so, Alice said. He's feeling better.

OK. Then let's go home, Lotte said. She pointed to the lift. I already said goodbye to him; we can leave.

They stopped at a petrol station halfway between the town and Lotte's house. Grass and nettles growing between the pumps; the windows of the kiosk where you paid were pasted over with black foil. The attendant came out of the door, yawning. Please fill the tank, Lotte said to the

Romanian. In the course of the day an unusual intimacy seemed to have developed between them, affection, a silent understanding. Wordless.

The Romanian took the money Lotte handed him; got out of the car, doing everything slowly as befitted the temperature, simple movements. Would you like some ice cream? Lotte asked Anna and Alice. Anna and Alice got out too. Lotte stayed in the car. Inside the kiosk cold air came out of the chest freezer like a net, palpable. A *cornetto*? Anna said, leaving the sliding door on the chest freezer open. Or an ice-lolly? The attendant drummed his thick fingers on the scuffed countertop, next to the cash register, worn from coins being pushed across it. Arabic music from a radio. Air-fresheners. Alice looked at the white BMW standing between the rusty petrol pumps, Lotte's unmoving profile unfocused behind the tinted windows. The Romanian had finished filling the tank. He was looking up at the mountain, holding his hand over his eyes, probably watching some bird, an eagle, a falcon, a buzzard. Under certain circumstances, Alice thought, you can feel jealous if another person merely looks up at the sky. She selected an ice-lolly and closed the freezer chest. The cashier pressed keys on his till. This, this, and that. Anything else?

The Romanian strolled in, put a banknote on the counter, chatted a little longer, *parlando*: *Come stai? Molto bene, grazie, arrividerci.* As always, Alice wouldn't touch the wooden stick of the ice-lolly, she had to wrap the paper cover around it. Sweet woodruff, raspberry, lemon. What flavour is it? the Romanian asked. *Dolomiti*, Alice said, as if he were hard of hearing. Anna belligerently showed the cashier her broken front tooth; inciting him. He banged shut the cash-register drawer so that it shook. In the car, Lotte smiled when they climbed in again. No sign of impatience. She was at peace with herself.

The last stretch was familiar. This village, the next village, the church tower, the Via dei Colli, then the Ristorante Nuovo Ponte, already familiar and consequently no longer of interest; they had sat there, so that was that, walked there, still beautiful, but no longer strange. And Lotte no longer gave them directions; she assumed the Romanian knew his way by now. The Romanian gently turned off the highway, the tic-tic-tic of the indicator, and then they were driving past the Nuovo Ponte which was not yet open for business, the chairs folded up and neatly placed against the tables under the blue awning. Then the road up to the five-way intersection and through the forged-iron gate, past the goats which didn't react in any way to the white BMW, and up to the stairs to Lotte and Conrad's house, next to which there was a space for the car, overgrown with blooming oleander. The Romanian parked the car in the space, just so, turned off the engine, and the hum of the air-conditioning faded and stopped. Gradually, one by one, outside noises came into the car. The bleating of a goat. The shrill call of a bird. Up in the house the telephone was ringing.

See you later, Lotte said. Thanks for coming with me. She climbed up the stairs, with deliberate haste, while the ringing in the house did not stop, the sound coming through the closed shutters. They could still hear it on their way to the yellow house, and it stopped only as Alice took the key from the flower box outside the kitchen window. Anna sat down on the bench, stretched out her legs and closed her eyes. Alice went into the kitchen and through the dining room and the living room to the French doors, pushed back the bolt, opened the doors wide, and stepped out on the terrace. Lizards darted across the tiles. Two butterflies rose up. The Romanian, close behind her, put his hand between Alice's shoulder blades. They stood there like that for a moment, undecided. Listening. Heard the car engine start up again, saw Lotte driving along the dirt road, past the goats, and through the gate. Then she was gone. Anna came out of the garden to the terrace stairs, and Alice took a step to one side.

Does that mean something. Anna said. What does it mean?

In the afternoon Alice retired to Conrad's room. She closed the shutters and lay down on the narrow bed without pulling the blanket over herself. It was dark except for one spot of light the size of a penny, a knothole through which the afternoon sun came in. The spot of light was golden. It wandered slowly along under the table and across the red carpet with its woven black pattern. A sundial. Alice lay there, her eyes open. She was thinking: Conrad had lain on this bed in this room with the shutters closed, back then, more than thirty years ago, when he was younger and the children were still small and the house on the hill was still a barn full of sheep and goats, when he was the same age as Alice was now – he had seen this spot of light wandering just as Alice now saw it wandering. Back then he had seen the same thing Alice saw now. Something significant seemed to be concealed behind this simple detail, and she couldn't immediately work out what it might be.

Something was going on outside; a car came, another drove away; the goats bleated excitedly and then fell silent again. Anna's voice on the terrace, the voice of the Romanian. Wind in the ivy outside the window. Very far away, on the lake, the howling roar of a speedboat motor. The Romanian and Anna wanted to go shopping. Lotte would return eventually. If something had happened Alice would find out, whatever it might be, and whether she wanted to or not.

Alice fell asleep. When she woke up again the spot of light was gone. She groped her way to the window and pushed open the shutters; the mountains on the other side of the lake glowed a faint pink; the sun was gone but it was still light.

Anna was lying on the bed, on the coverlet printed with fig leaves. She was lying on her side, sound asleep. Alice tiptoed downstairs and found the Romanian in the kitchen. They had obviously been shopping; the refrigerator was crammed full, on the pantry shelves there were many small bottles containing a red liquid, net bags of lemons.

What's that?

Aperol.

It's what we were supposed to drink in Salò.

In the freezer compartment, water was freezing in little pink and blue moulds, hearts and shells. The whole kitchen smelled of basil, olives, sage.

This kitchen has everything you need, the Romanian said. This family has thought of everything. Lotte's thought of everything. Would you like a coffee?

Oh yes, Alice said. I'd like that.

Her eyelids felt swollen, and she was tired, as if drugged; it was impossible to leave the Romanian. She would have liked to cling to him, she *had* to stay with him in the kitchen, to be near him. She pulled a stool over to the kitchen door and sat down, half in, half out, her back against the wall. Countless ants were scurrying across the threshold. The Romanian put a cup of coffee into her empty hand. She gazed out into the garden, towards the evening-tinged mountains, back to the kitchen and the Romanian who, barefoot on the red and white tiles, was cutting the melon Conrad had put into the refrigerator, first in half, then quarters, and then slices. The juice of the melon ran over his wrists. He was humming. *Io cerco la Titina, Titina, Titina*. A little old man came walking up the dirt road. Barely lifting his feet. Walked past Lotte and Conrad's house, on to the yellow house, towards them.

Someone's coming, Alice said.

The Romanian nodded. I think it's the gardener. He was with the goats before and mowing the lawn, and he took something up to Lotte.

Alice got up. The old man was walking slowly and calmly, his eyes fixed on the ground, his hands in the pockets of his black trousers. He wore a sleeveless white undershirt and a straw hat. Alice closed her eyes. Maybe he'd be gone when she opened them again. Fata Morgana. He was the messenger bringing news. She opened her eyes; by then he was nearly at the door.

The Romanian soundlessly put the knife with which he'd been slicing the melon on the cutting board. He wiped his hands and wrists on his torn jeans. Alice looked at him. Then she turned and looked at the old man. The old man took his hands out of his pockets and with his left hand took off his straw hat. Snow-white hair. He said, *Lui è morto. Signor Conrad è morto.*

What did he say, Alice said. She had understood what he said; but even if she hadn't understood the words, she would have understood the gestures he made: the old man, with the straw hat under his arm, had raised his hands, showing them the calloused hard palms. Empty and white.

Alice stepped out into the garden. The Romanian did too. The old man moved aside, giving them room. The three of them stood next to each other. The old man said something; the Romanian nodded, *Sì, sì,* yes, yes, *capito,* he had understood. The old man shook hands with him, then with Alice. With a motion of his head he took in everything around him: the olive grove, the wall, the house, the oleander, the orange trees, the silent, slender cypress.

He said, *Vita brutta.*

Again Alice said, What did he say.

And the Romanian replied, repeating what he said, He said – Ugly life. That's what he said.

Next morning Alice went up to Lotte's house.

The three outside doors all led into the same room. The room was large and dim; behind some screens a bed perhaps, perhaps it was the bed Conrad had been lying in with a fever, a tropical infection. His heart had beaten too fast for too long. Lying in this bed he had heard them arrive, Alice and the friends he didn't know. The Romanian and the dark Anna, both of whom he never got to know, which was too bad but didn't matter at all. Fever. Alice's voice through the half-open door. We're here now, Lotte, and we're very happy to be here. Lotte's voice.

Lotte was upstairs. Alice went up the spiral staircase to the upper floor; the shutters were wide open, the glass doors were pushed aside, everything was light and bright, and the view extended far across the lake. Lotte was sitting at a table by the window. A German newspaper lay on the table. A silver letter opener. A bowl of eggs, a bowl of zucchini blossoms. Lotte, pointing to the eggs and the blossoms, said, Fulvio brought them, our gardener; look, isn't that nice? She was pale, tall, and tired. She sat ramrod straight and looked questioningly at Alice for a while, as if waiting for something to occur to her, as if trying to remember something. Then it came to her – Alice, dear. She pushed the chair next to her away from the table and Alice sat down. They sat like this, next to each other, in silence for a while. Then Alice said, Lotte, you must tell us what we should do. Should we leave or stay, I don't know what we should do.

Oh, you ought to stay a little longer, Lotte said. Stay. It's good for me if you stay, why should you leave now. Your friend is very nice. He can take me to the hospital, and pick me up. You ought to stay. Conrad would have wanted that too.

Not looking at Alice she said, You're the last person who spoke to him, you know that.

Yes, Alice said. I know.

And how did that go, Lotte said.

He said he had thought he was invulnerable, Alice said. Grateful that she was able to say that much, and grateful that Lotte now laughed, softly, but still.

He said that Lotte said. She shook her head.

That's what he said, Alice said.

They have laid him out in the hospital; that's one of the good things about Italy. I'll go there and sit with him. There are other dead people in the room too, a small chapel, other families, it's actually quite wonderful. He can stay there like that for two days. Or three. Wouldn't you like to go with me?

No, Alice said. No. I can't.

All right, Lotte said. It doesn't matter. You don't have to.

Come with me, Lotte said, I want to show you something.

They stood next to each other on the large terrace with the chair and the stone sphere. Lotte pulled the green hose from the drum, turned on the water. She aimed the broadly fanned glistening stream into the lavender bushes; it took a little while. Lotte said, Wait. Then cardinal beetles began pouring out of the lavender bushes by the hundreds, a red-and-black-spotted flood of fleeing insects, seemingly endless. They inundated the terrace, running in all directions.

Look at that, Lotte said. Just look at that.

In the middle of the night, long past midnight, maybe already in the grey of dawn, the Romanian went up the stairs from the terrace to the first floor in the yellow house, past his own room and up to the second floor, through Anna's room, into Alice's room. Conrad's room. Alice's room. He closed the door softly behind him. The room was dark because Alice had closed the shutters tight. In the dark the Romanian groped his way to Alice's bed. The narrow bed with the metal frame. Alice stretched her hand out to him; it was the most affectionate of gestures. Because she knew that this would be the most affectionate gesture, she guided her hand as explicitly as possible, explicitly for her and explicitly for the Romanian, whose hand was small and familiar. She couldn't see his face. He couldn't see hers. She took his hand with all the expressiveness she had. Drew him to her. The rest was rough and angry, unrestrained.

That afternoon they took a boat. Anna, Alice, and the Romanian. They had only a few days left, but no one cared. The lake remained dark blue, ice cold, sometimes misty, occasionally a clear view. Aggressive swans, ducks with four, five, six, or seven ducklings, the water always soft. Every hour the ferry went from west to east and back again, and the pebbles on the beach got hotter and hotter. That afternoon Anna wore a grey dress with green flowers, sandals with cork heels, her hair in a child's pigtail. Alice wore a white blouse and a lilac-coloured skirt. The

Romanian had on a light-coloured shirt and the torn jeans with traces of melon juice on the seams. The boy at the boat-rental place next to the Mussolini villa with the pretentious view of Monte Baldo and its cloud-enveloped peak felt he had to finish his apple and fling the core to the swans before he could hand over the oars for a boat. A flag hung limply in the shadow of his little boathouse, and the clanking of the chain with which the boats were tied together scared away the swans. The Romanian rowed the boat out of the little harbour, confidently and almost elegantly. Alice saw the boy raise his eyebrows before he sank back into his plastic chair. The Romanian rowed the boat far out, probably dangerously far out; there was no one there who could have told them anything about it, but they could clearly feel the current. A wind had come up, water splashed into the boat, they were all quite exhausted anyway. The Romanian ignored Anna's oblique references to their distance from shore, showing a casual indifference that didn't suit him.

Who'll go swimming?

Not me, Alice said.

With his back to Anna and Alice, the Romanian took off his shirt, then his jeans. Standing naked in the prow of the boat he bent his knees for a moment. Alice looked at him, his back, his arms. Narrow shoulders, slender neck. Bite marks, scratches. Black and blue marks all over. Then he jumped into the water, dived down, and was gone.

Good heavens, Anna said, raising her hand to her mouth; she was truly shocked. Good heavens. Did I do that?

An insect had drowned in the milky foam of Alice's *latte macchiato* on the terrace of the café in Salò. Alice had felt it on her tongue – very light, a multi-legged body concealed in the white foam. Gagging, she'd spat it out, sticking her tongue far out, had spat it back onto the spoon. What are you doing there? Anna asked, leaning forward, interested and sympathetic but disgusted at the same time.

Alice said, If it's a spider, I'll scream. It wasn't a spider. It was something else, maybe a cricket, or a cicada? Small, black, cute, with little bent legs and a shiny abdomen. *Il caldo, il tempo*, the waiter had said, pointing up into the sky, shrugging and removing the plate, the spoon, the foam and the little animal from the table. Didn't bring another coffee. Maybe I almost swallowed a cricket, a cicada, a head-cricket, Alice thought. What was the difference between them again? Conrad would surely have known. But Conrad was *morto. Lui è morto.* He was being taken to Germany by cargo carrier across the Alps, in July of all times.

Strange. Anna said, We didn't even get to know Conrad, the Romanian and I, we never even saw him. What was he like? What had he been like?

While ... To think that while they had stopped at the petrol station, and while the Romanian was looking up into the sky at a falcon, an eagle, or a buzzard. While Alice was sliding open the top of the chest freezer, and Anna said the word *cornetto*, and the gas station attendant was drumming with his fingers on the counter and Lotte was sitting in the

car, unmoving behind the tinted windows, her profile outlined against the mountain, and Alice's hand was deep in
the chest freezer, in slow motion tearing open a cardboard
box full of ice-lollies, raspberry, lemon and sweet woodruff
– What flavour is it? the Romanian had asked. And Alice
had replied *Dolomiti* – Conrad had passed away. In a hot
room at the end of a corridor with glittering light, his heart
had at first fibrillated and then stopped beating, just like
that, and no goodbye, that was all. While they paid, walked
out into the dusty plaza in front of the petrol pumps, nettles
and grass growing between the stones. Thinking about it.
Over and over again. I can't tell you what Conrad was like.
I can no longer tell you.

One afternoon Alice packed her suitcases, then sat down
for a long time on the chair at Conrad's table, gazing at
the guest book, finally took the pen and managed to draw
a dash on the paper; even that was embarrassing. Drinking a last Aperol on the terrace with the red cushions, the
cold-blooded lizards, the unbearably beautiful view of the
landscape. The Romanian and his indifferent, unchanging
politeness. Should I marry you now or what; but we're much
too old to get married – Alice asked herself and came to no
conclusion. Go for another swim. One last time. Sandals
in hand, she walked to the little dock near the wall and
the gate to the overgrown garden. When Alice, alone on
the beach, undressed completely, and went cautiously into
the water, tripping on the slippery stones, she remembered
what Conrad had said about the lake, back then when he

invited her to come for a visit. He had said, the lake was always ice cold, she would have to force herself to go into the water. He had said, But you'll go into the water in spite of that. And you won't regret it. You'll never regret it.

What did he mean by that? And what did it mean for everything else? Alice's feet left the bottom; she dove down and swam out.

III

Richard

Margaret phoned saying she needed cigarettes and water. Otherwise nothing, but she really did need the cigarettes and the water. It was urgent.

What kind of cigarettes?

Those long, slender ones, for women; Slims. And carbonated water.

Nothing else, really?

No, really, nothing else. Thanks.

I'll be over in about an hour, Alice said. I'll hurry.

It was an afternoon in early summer. A Saturday. Actually Alice *had* been intending to do something else, nothing specific, just something else. It was also Raymond's day off.

I have to go now, she said to Raymond, and Raymond who was lying on the bed, reading, only nodded absent-mindedly and didn't ask any questions. She put on flat shoes and a light-coloured jacket. She didn't really need the jacket, didn't know when she'd be back, maybe late; it might be colder by then. She stood next to the bed, looking down at Raymond's bare back, at the band of tattooing on his left arm, decorations and words in indigo blue on his always-pale skin. She said, Raymond – he turned round – I'm leaving now.

He nodded. Don't come back too late. Give them my best wishes.

Alice put on her sunglasses before she stepped outside. She hadn't been out of the house all day. The street was teeming with people; she held her breath. Lots of people, sitting at long rows of tables under awnings or sun umbrellas beneath the heavy green trees. Talking to one another, without let-up. Nodding, talking, gesticulating people. Loud laughter. The wooden ship in the middle of the park was occupied by a cluster of children. Crying, screaming, overheated children. A nimbus of mothers sitting on benches surrounding the ship. Alice walked by, her hands in the pockets of her too-warm jacket; there were coins in the pockets, her keys, the cellphone, an old movie ticket, sweet wrappers. The sound of basketballs hitting the fence of the basketball court, a sound that, now that it was summertime, could sometimes be heard as early as six in the morning – at six a.m. somebody was already on the court tossing a ball into the basket or against the fence, again and again. Sometimes it woke Alice up. Still tired but astonished at the morning light on the white walls of the room.

The way to Margaret's, to Margaret and Richard's, led past the flower stand in the Prenzlauer Allee station. The station hall was large, and there under its arched windows were flowers in plastic vases, an amphitheatre of flowers, in front of which, on a folding chair in the exact centre, sat the Vietnamese flower seller. Sitting there day in and day out. The hall was shadowy; the colours of the flowers were dark, the dark white of lilies, the dark pink of gerbera daisies, and dark iris purple. Chamomile. Snapdragons. Sunflowers. The Vietnamese flower seller was asleep. She slept the sleep of travellers; whenever her head would fall to one side, she would straighten up again with her eyes still closed. In her dreams, Alice thought, the trains come and go; it must be a constant vague noise. Alice stood there, undecided; waking up the flower seller was out of the question. Actually she didn't want to bring any flowers today, only water and cigarettes, nothing else. There was nothing else she could bring them.

The last time she visited Richard and Margaret she'd bought peonies at this same stand, having first thought about it for a long time: Seven peonies, please, and don't add anything. An uneven number, a superstition. Five were too few, and she didn't have enough money for nine. Richard didn't have a vase. Margaret, who was now staying with Richard all the time in his apartment and never far from his bed, had put the peonies into a milk bottle and pointed out to Richard how beautiful they were. Richard said peonies were his favourite flowers. Alice believed him; he wouldn't have said it if she'd brought him narcissus or tulips. A coincidence. All three were pleased about it. How long ago was that? Two weeks. It was two weeks ago. Richard had got out of bed; they'd been able to sit in the living room together for an hour. At the oval table in front of a shelf full of books. Richard sat with his back to the books. He was wearing pyjamas and whenever Margaret asked him to, he drank from a glass of water. He was smoking slowly and carefully; too late to stop, it would have made no sense for him to give up smoking now. Alice sat facing him, Margaret between them. Margaret talked, crying and smiling through her tears. Richard didn't take his eyes off her. As if that were what he still had to do – to look at Margaret.

When she came back from this visit, Alice had asked Raymond, Would you rather die before me or after me? After you, I think, Raymond had said. It had taken a while before he could answer; he seemed to consider the question itself impossible. Why? He asked. He wasn't quite sure. And you?

She'd shaken her head and put her hand over his mouth. She couldn't answer him.

Alice crossed the intersection, obeying the signals; there were days when she felt she had to be careful, to be more cautious than usual. She couldn't say where that came from. Raymond, too, had days like that. Both of them did.

Take care of yourself.

And you take care too.

She waited for the light to turn green; then she walked on. On her left the tram. Overhead the elevated train, rumbling downward, underground. Cars stopped in choreographed rows, seemingly meaningful, following a synchronised set of rules. Beautiful light signals. Above it all, the pale sky. Alice took off her sunglasses and used her elbow to push open the door to the newsagent's. Barricades of plastic boxes full of sweets. Vampire teeth, white mice, liquorice snails, and behind them the shop's fat proprietor, feeble movements, breathing and rustling, a heavy animal in its cave. Drums containing lottery tickets. Boxes of chocolate bars, bags of sweets, chocolate surprise eggs. Information, advice, little blinking bulbs, announcements. You could put all this on exhibition, Raymond would say when he stood inside shops like this. Just as it is, transport it to a museum. Alice put some paper money on the little tray in the middle of everything and said, Two packs of Slims, please. It had been years since she last bought cigarettes, and her hands trembled. Two bottles of water? The fat newsagent pointed wordlessly to a shelf next to the counter, and Alice picked out two bottles of Spree Spring Water from among the seven varieties. Did Margaret want the water for herself or for Richard? And did it matter? She wasn't sure. It could all be very important or not important at all.

The bottles were plastic. Tinted blue. Spring water.

A bag?

Yes, please.

He pushed an orange-coloured bag across the counter, counted out the clinking change into the little tray, and withdrew behind the plastic boxes.

Even as she was standing there facing him she couldn't say any more what he actually looked like. Broken fingernails. The hem of his sweater frayed. The shop smelling of potting soil and wet paper. She said, Have a good day, said it just to hear how he would answer. He said, The same to you. Said it in an absolutely flat voice. Alice pulled open the door and, with the bag containing the two bottles and cigarette packs pressed to her chest, she turned left and walked down the street.

Along Rheinsberger Strasse. Rheinsberger was a quiet street, in contrast to the street where Alice lived. A simple, quiet, beautiful street, no more, no less. Old acacia trees on both sides, cobblestone pavement, A patchwork quilt of asphalt – light-coloured asphalt, dark-coloured asphalt, seams of tar. On Rheinsberger you could walk along the middle of the traffic lane. Alice walked down the middle with her orange bag, the spring water and cigarettes. A gentle wind moved through the acacias shaking the leaves; light flickered through them onto the asphalt. From the open windows, the sound of televisions, the ringing of telephones, the smell of food, popular songs from radios. A street on a Saturday afternoon in June. Alice thought the street had a Sunday air to it, something about it reminded her of childhood Sundays, of the long drawn-out summer Sundays pulsing with something – as if it were that time just before the onset of a thunderstorm. Waiting for it to come. Waiting for the thunderstorm.

The house where Richard lived was on the right-hand side of the street. The right-hand side was in the shade. Alice looked up at Richard's closed windows and thought: In a room in that apartment in this house on this street a man I know is dying. Everyone else is doing something else. Thinking this was a little like reciting a poem, someone else's words, not anything you could comprehend. She stopped under the arch of the main entrance and listened to a faraway child's recorder: Cuckoo, cuckoo, half a scale, two trills, and it was finished. Alice pressed the bell. Leaning against the door, she pressed the copper bell button with her index finger. The buzzer buzzed, and the door opened.

The peonies in the milk bottle were wilted but still standing on the windowsill. A white-edged blue tablecloth covered the table, on it a bottle of water, an ashtray, an open address book with the telephone on top, a stationery pad, pens, matches, a pair of reading glasses. Margaret fetched two glasses from the kitchen, emptied the ashtray. She sat down where Richard had sat two weeks ago, on the chair in front of the books, in the shelter of the books, their spines, their consolingly familiar titles. Who would read these thousand books once Richard no longer needed them? These were the very questions Alice was ashamed of, but which she kept thinking anyway. Margaret poured Alice a glass of water, then one for herself. She opened a pack of cigarettes.

Alice could still remember just what that was like, each detail – tugging gently on the little strip of cellophane, then the rustling foil, prying out the first cigarette. Virginia and orient tobaccos – one world. Margaret lit a cigarette, blew out the match, getting rid of the sulphur smell with a wave of her hand. Her face was tanned by the June sun. There was something radiant, strong, very much alive about her. She smoked cheerfully. It's nice that you came, Alice, she said. And suddenly Alice also thought that it was nice to be allowed to sit here again so unexpectedly, in this room, whose permanence would end at the exact moment Richard stopped breathing, but no one knew just when that would happen, and as long as he was still breathing, it was all here: the table, the books, the flowers, the reading glasses, the glasses of water, his name on the door, and his brown jacket hanging over the back of the desk chair.

Margaret, Alice said.

Margaret nodded, said, Well, as far as possible we've worked it all out. We've arranged everything. The musicians, the cemetery chapel, the gravesite. We've set a date for the funeral. In three weeks.

And what if Richard hasn't died by then, Alice asked.

Oh, by then he'll have managed that, Margaret said.

They'd discussed the subject two weeks ago; Margaret and Richard had talked about it in front of Alice. Alice had listened. At first she thought it was indecent, unseemly, to be talking with Richard about his own funeral, but instead it turned out to be the natural thing to do. Not unseemly.

Richard had said he wanted his friends to carry his coffin, not the gravediggers. No sermon by a minister, no quotations. If the weather's good, that would please him. Margaret had taken notes on the stationery pad: Whom to call, who should be there, no one should stay away. The food: sandwiches with plum jam, meatballs, and beer.

She had said, That's what we'll do. We'll do it just like that, Richard; it'll be a very nice funeral, and Richard had said, Yes it will be, and he had looked at Margaret, a look that Alice tried to describe to Raymond later, but had to give up on because it was impossible to describe.

That's how it is, Margaret said. I haven't slept for a whole week. I've distanced myself; I'm standing above it all. When it's over I'll collapse. I realise that. Hardly anyone has come to see us since your visit two weeks ago. Things went downhill fast after that. Hard to believe how fast they can go downhill. You can see it happening. You can actually see it.

She stopped talking and listened. Now he's asleep, she said. He's not in pain. What time is it? Let's see – almost five. That means the nurse will be here soon, in half an hour; he's got a suitcase full of morphine that he carries around with him through half the city. Will you stay a while longer?

Yes, Alice said. I'll stay. She looked across the hall to the other room that faced the courtyard. Richard's bed was next to the wall on the right. The window was open, the curtains drawn. Richard was lying there with his head near the door, his closed eyes turned towards the window. Alice could see his head, the grey hair.

Margaret said, The curtains are from when I was a girl.

Muslin, Alice said.

Yes, muslin. Margaret nodded. If I had known as a girl – fifty years ago – that one day I'd be hanging them in Richard's death chamber. Or …

The white curtains swayed gently in the breeze. Almost imperceptibly, back and forth. Causing a slight change in the light. Hints of embroidery, trimmings. Tiny flowers circled by wreaths, various shades of white.

The visiting nurse came at six. He brought papaya, mango, and pineapple in a little plastic container, all cut into small pieces. And more water. The room was warm, summery. For a while, they sat there together. Eating the papaya, mango, pineapple. You've got to eat, Margaret, the nurse said, preparing the morphine and charging the syringe. Then he went into the bedroom. Alice picked up a piece of papaya, smooth and orange coloured. She heard the nurse speaking to Richard, calmly and matter-of-factly, not as if he were talking to a child. She glanced over briefly; he was bending over the bed, had put his hands on Richard's head. It looked as though he were going to kiss him. Then he came back and, sitting at the table, tied the laces of his trainers. He was still fairly young. Shaved head, soft features, several earrings. To Margaret he said, So, I'll have my cellphone with me; we'll be on the roof today, grilling and stuff, I'll probably have a beer. Or two. Nothing's going to happen today. Maybe tomorrow. I think, tomorrow it will all be over. But call me if you need me.

He said, He notices when you're sitting next to him, when you touch him. He notices everything. Maybe he was saying this to Alice. They said goodbye, formally, it didn't matter that they didn't know each other. Then he left.

At some point Alice left too. Margaret walked her to the door; they held each other in a brief, tight hug. I'll let you know, Margaret said. When it happens. When it's over, I mean. I'll call you.

Alice went back along Rheinsberger Strasse, walking down the middle of the street, on the light-coloured, the dark-coloured asphalt. Dusk was falling, and lights were going on in the houses, people were watering their plants on the balconies, and the water dripped down on the shady pavements. The hum of evening. The dog days of summer. It hadn't rained in a long time and dried linden blossoms rustled in the gutters. Very gradually the heat was letting up a bit. Cars at the traffic lights on the main street, the elevated train going in the opposite direction, and the tram with its green windowpanes and the blue sparks flying in the grid under the bridge. Alice passed the newsagent's, its window pasted over with ads, the ugly newspaper racks, and the neon sign for Toto-Lotto now on, flickering. A loose connection. The fat man was standing in front of the door. He had come outside, just for a change. Hands in his trouser pockets, the frayed sweater, a friendly, tired face. He nodded at Alice, and Alice nodding back, thought, He knows where I've been. No, he can't know. The water's been drunk; the cigarettes will all have been smoked by tomorrow morning.

She stopped at the traffic lights and phoned Raymond. He answered after the seventh ring, and his voice sounded far away and strange.

Alice.

Would you please be sitting downstairs when I come home? Alice cleared her throat. She looked at the big intersection, and for a second she had the feeling that she had lost track of the meaning of everything. As though everything was dissolving and re-forming differently with a new meaning. Scribbles. Acoustic scrawls. She pressed her eyes closed with her left hand. The feeling went away. She said, I don't know, am I interrupting something?

No, Raymond said. You're not interrupting anything. Are you saying I should go down to the bar? In front of the house?

It would be nice, Alice said. What are you doing right now?

Reading, Raymond said. He laughed. Oh well. Actually I was sleeping. I'll go downstairs. See you soon.

See you soon, Alice said.

The street was still full of people. Talking constantly. No end in sight, no final word. But now that it was getting dark, everything sounded more muted. Lanterns on the tables. Men and women sitting across from each other. Heavy green trees. Bicycles, locked together along the edge of the pavement, the moon above the park, the ship, empty now, an empty wooden ship with an openwork railing in a sea of sand. The benches all around it, deserted. Paper cups, newspapers, bottles. Bottle collectors emerging from the bushes, polite and quiet, picking up the bottles, letting others go first. Bats among the trees. Swifts, their angry, crazy screams. The ping-pong of table-tennis balls, cell-phone tunes, symphonies. Alice walked along the edge of the park towards the house where she lived, where Raymond had been sleeping and reading that afternoon and early evening. On the first floor the light was on, also on the third floor, and there was a light in her window. Before going downstairs Raymond had turned on the little light near the window for Alice. She could see him now. He was sitting in front of the house, under the blue awning of the bar, at the last in a long row of tables, right next to the front door of their house. His back was to the wine-red house wall; he was drinking a small beer. His jacket was draped over the back of the chair next to him. Alice almost stopped walking. She tried an old game – to see him as if she didn't know him. As if he were just anyone. As if she were seeing him for the first time. What would she think of him? What did he actually look like? It didn't work. She gave up.

'Evening, the waitress said.

'Evening, Raymond answered for Alice, inimitable, it sounded exactly right.

Tired?

Yes, I'm a little tired, Alice said. I'll have a small beer too, please.

The waitress smiled, first at Raymond, then at Alice, then up at the sky. She stood there with them a little longer. Like Raymond, she had a tattoo, a Mexican sun on her back, in the exact centre between her shoulder blades. Sometimes when Alice ran into her in the hallway of the house, they would ask each other, How are you? Thanks, pretty good. Lots of work. Always a lot of work. Never enough time. No time. Time for what, actually? They agreed that they didn't quite know what for.

The waitress was the same one who, every morning, wrote, *Happy Hour* on the blackboard next to the front door of the bar. Above that, she drew a smiling moon face. Day after day. She knocked lightly on the table with her knuckles, then she walked away. Alice and Raymond didn't often sit at the bar in front of the house.

Alice took off her jacket and sat down next to Raymond. They sat there next to each other and watched the people walking to the left across the park, to the right down the street.

Are you hungry? Raymond asked. Would you like something to eat?

I'm not hungry, Alice said. I already had something to eat. Mango and papaya and pineapple. It sounded funny. She thought of the male nurse who was now sitting on some rooftop in a folding chair, grilling and stuff, with a view of the entire shining, glittering city, holding his third bottle of beer, his cellphone in his pocket. Margaret might call him. Margaret might call Alice, too. The nurse had had very dark eyes, somewhat distant, serious.

Alice said, He's become inconceivably small. I mean Richard. He's become as small as a child these past two weeks. His skin is yellow. It's all over, but his heart is still beating; it simply keeps on beating.

He wasn't conscious this time, Raymond said. Or was he?

No, Alice said. He isn't conscious any more. But the nurse thinks he notices everything. Could be; I'm not sure. How would he know? I touched Richard. He sighed. Is that a reaction?

Yes, Raymond said, that's a reaction.

Maybe, Alice said.

The waitress set the beer down in front of Alice. Golden, in a tall glass on a beer mat that Alice pushed away after the waitress had left. The beer was ice-cold and sweet. What was it you were reading? Alice asked.

Science fiction, Raymond said. He looked happy. Some great parts in it about rain.

He didn't say anything more. Neither did Alice. It was quite all right this way. Most likely the nurse wouldn't have said anything either. At least nothing about Richard, about other things, yes – football news, polar bears, weather forecasts, the presidential elections.

Margaret had said, After you leave I'll put the folding cot next to Richard's bed. And lie down next to him. I won't sleep, I'll just lie there. So she was now lying on the folding cot next to Richard's bed in the room with the white muslin curtains of her girlhood, and so on and so forth. Until Richard was gone. One's girlhood, What is all the rest, then. Alice wondered.

She thought of Margaret. Of the male nurse. Of Rheinsberger Strasse and about the Sundays of her own childhood ... When a blind man with a hurdy-gurdy and a little monkey on a rusty chain had sung in the rear courtyard; she'd been allowed to throw coins wrapped in newspaper out of the kitchen window – when she told this to Raymond he hadn't believed her. But why not? She also thought about Richard, but in a different way. She looked past Raymond and the dark park; far away, a late-night plane rose into the sky, and she remembered that Raymond, on one of the first nights they had sat together like this, had said the sound of a plane at night made him sad. Why? Alice had asked. Because it's as if it were the last possible plane. For me, Raymond had said, and Alice had understood a part of it and a part of it she didn't understand, and something of what he said had also caused her to feel hurt. She was reminded of all this whenever she saw a plane at night. Whether she wanted to or not, she remembered it every time. A sort of price to pay. But for what?

Will you be going there again? Raymond asked.

No, Alice said. I think today was the last time.

Sunday, they drove into the country. With the Sunday paper, a tartan blanket, a Thermos of tea, three apples, and a bottle of water. Northward. On a secondary road. They parked at the edge of the forest, then walked into the forest on a sandy path until they reached the lake. Alice dawdled, walking quite a way behind Raymond; sometimes he was out of sight, then again there he would be in front of her on the path and in the middle of the light slanting down through the pine trees brightly illuminating something seemingly insubstantial. Fat bugs waddled along at the edge of the path, persistently and stubbornly. Somewhere a woodpecker was pecking. Raymond was far ahead of her. They walked around the lake, looking for a place to spread out their blanket. It was important to Alice, Raymond didn't care. They couldn't find a spot for the blanket, only bumpy, swampy grass, criss-crossed by tree roots. So they were left with no choice but to stay in the shade, close to the trees, Alice leaning her back against a tree trunk, her feet almost in the water. The water was green, muddy, and warm.

Raymond went swimming; Alice read the Sunday paper without understanding a single word, without wanting to understand. The rustling of the pages. Frogs in the wet sand. At a safe distance from the shore the unpleasantly small head of a water snake. Some birds Alice did not recognise flying above the lake. Kites? She'd always found the name intriguing, had never known what the bird itself looked like. Was she mistaken? Alice shrugged, yes, possibly. Raymond came back, breathing the way you breathe when you're just coming out of the water; he dried himself, looked back at the distance he'd swum.

Was it nice?

Well, of course. Aren't you going in?

I'll see, Alice said.

Raymond drank some tea, ate an apple, opened the newspaper. Alice watched as a mosquito settled on his left shoulder, pushed its proboscis under his skin, and pumped with the hind part of its body, calmly and for a long time. She watched Raymond reading, his chin resting in his hand. He was elsewhere, in a parallel world; twice he smiled at something. Then he folded the paper, got up, and stretched until his bones cracked. Bent his head to the right and to the left, the neck vertebrae cracking. He said, I'll take a turn around the lake, disappearing between the black yet simultaneously bright tree trunks. Blotches of light in the grass. Busy ants, wasps around the remains of his apple, the tea in the tin cup, cold. Alice fell asleep, in a second-long dream the male nurse put away all the things on the table in Richard's room, then pulled off the blue tablecloth, doing it all with a distinctly chilly 'that's-how-things-stand' expression. She was startled awake as her head fell to one side like the Vietnamese flower seller's had in the hall of the Prenzlauer Allee train station. Raymond was standing with his feet in the water, looking out across the dark lake. He said, We have to leave, Alice. I'm on the night shift today. Clouds covered the sun. It had suddenly turned cool. Even as the nurse in the dream had been picking up Richard's glasses.

Alice packed up. They shook out the blanket together, threw the remains of the apples into the reeds. Folded up the crumpled, messy newspaper. The paper seemed to have doubled in size. I'll be right there, Alice said. That old disquiet on excursions, at the end always sentimental and wistful, as if it had been their last, as if it might have been their last. She hadn't gone swimming. Should she have? She should have done everything differently, not just today, but always. Done everything differently. She walked behind Raymond on the path, then she walked beside him, took his hand; they held hands the rest of the way. He was carrying the basket; she, the blanket and the newspaper. They met no one.

What sort of arrangement did you make with Margaret? Raymond asked.

He had suddenly remembered again.

She'll call me, Alice said. She'll phone when it's over.

Half an hour in a traffic jam on the motorway. Alice took off her shoes, put her feet up on the dashboard as she used to do fifteen years ago, fiddled with the radio and rolled down the window. At the side of the road a strip of shoulder, cornfields, windmills. At the far end of the twinkling chain of cars, the silhouette of the TV tower. Both of them looked at it. Raymond turned off the radio, then the engine. He looked at his watch and made an involuntary irritable sound. They had left in good time; he wouldn't be late, yet in spite of that he was on edge. Alice wondered whether she ought to tell him about her dream. But she was afraid of its interpretation, not what it would say about Raymond, but about herself. She unbuckled her seat belt, took her feet off the dashboard. She said, You got sunburned. Raymond said, I know.

On the other side of the motorway, an occasional car drove by, heading north. We should have taken the secondary road. Probably wouldn't have been any better. The windmills turned slowly, casting strange rotating shadows in the dry fields. Raymond started the engine again. They were both tired. Then the traffic jam dissolved.

The apartment was as quiet as if they'd been away a long time. The kitchen window facing the courtyard was wide open; Alice watered the flowers on the windowsill. Flowers with blue leaves whose name she didn't know. Raymond didn't either. Thirteen blue leaves and a little flower head on each one. Alice had counted them. Tiny spiders had woven their webs between the stems. The mercury in the thermometer on the house wall above the flower box stood at 27 °C. A pale half moon was already visible in the sky. Signs of a thunderstorm above the rooftops, absolutely no wind now.

And what else are you doing today. Tonight.

Raymond was standing in the doorway to the kitchen; he'd taken a shower and put on another T-shirt; his skin was slightly reddened, and there were faint rings under his eyes. The T-shirt covered the tattoo on his left arm: 'The last shall be the first.' Alice was as afraid of the meaning of this tattoo as of the meaning of her dreams. Years ago she had asked Raymond not to tell her why he had had this sentence tattooed in calligraphy on his arm, and Raymond had promised not to. He had kept his promise.

I'm not doing anything, she said.

She was standing by the kitchen window holding the bottle of water for the flowers; she looked at Raymond; there would be nothing he could say, but for one moment she did look at him the way she felt – helpless and close to tears.

What should I do? I'll wait for Margaret's phone call. I keep thinking about it. I'm thinking about it now. At the lake I didn't think so much about it. It's not bad; don't worry about me. I'll just stay home.

She shook her head. Set the water bottle down on the windowsill. There seemed to be something about her that kept Raymond from touching her, from putting his arms around her – how do you say it – she couldn't think of the word embrace; she wished he would go now.

Till tomorrow morning, Raymond said. He gave her a searching look.

Yes, till tomorrow morning.

Call me if Margaret phones.

I will, Alice said.

Promise.

Sure. She walked him to the door. Then went across the hall to the bedroom. Pulled up the blinds, opened the window, and leaned out. It took a while. Sometimes it took so long that Alice thought he would never come out. And what then?

Raymond stepped out of the house. His jacket slung over his shoulder. He disappeared from sight under the awning, emerged again at the corner of the street, crossed at the intersection. He went over to the other side of the street and walked along the edge of the park. Just as Alice had yesterday on her way to Margaret and Richard's. Had Raymond watched her yesterday?

She hadn't turned round. Now, she could see Raymond walking – among all those people on the street, in the park, in the cafés, at the tables in the shade of the trees, he was the one she knew and knew about yet didn't understand. He turned round, looked up at their apartment, raised his hand, and waved. Alice waved back. Then he was gone. She kept looking out of the window for a while longer. The last of the children left the park; the street lights went on. In the basketball court, hidden by the leaves of the trees, someone was still throwing a ball into the basket, again and again. Open windows, profusely planted balconies, and the water from the flowers dripping down on the pavement. A ring of fiery clouds around the sun hanging low in the sky. Tomorrow was Monday. Alice closed the window. She lowered the blind, searched for the phone, and found it on the floor beside the bed, next to Raymond's open book. *The street lamps buckled weakly, newsstands and advertising columns dissolved into the air, everything everywhere crackled, hissed, and rustled, became porous and transparent, turned into little piles of dust, and disappeared. In the distance the outlines of the Town Hall tower became blurry and blended with the blue sky. For a while the old tower clock, detached from everything else, still hung suspended in the sky until it too vanished.* Alice took the book and the phone and went back to the kitchen. Pulling a chair over to the table, she sat down, placed the phone next to the book, and continued reading.

IV

Malte

It was raining the day Alice saw Frederick for the first and only time. A light rain but steady – diagonal lines against the winter sky. Mid-November. Frederick had said he was coming to Berlin anyway; he hadn't picked this weather for their meeting; neither had Alice, although it was the sort of weather that made her feel good. Reason enough to feel sleepy and lethargic, rain enough for an umbrella. As usual, her car was parked far away, umpteen streets away, at the edge of the district. Alice left the house too early, carrying an umbrella, wearing high heels, a grey coat, her bag slung over one shoulder, and feeling as if she were dressed for a state visit. On a whim, Frederick had taken a hotel room in the centre of the city, right by the river. Alice thought of it as a whim, but it might simply have been practical, a room downtown. With a view of the water and a steel bridge with pigeons nesting in its struts and trains rolling across from east to west and back. Milky green water with shimmering streaks of oil. The beautiful River Spree, its rusty freight barges, excursion boats, shabby tugboats, everything the same today as it had been forty years ago. Maybe Frederick chose the location because of that.

Alice was to pick him up at the hotel, around eleven.

In your room?

In the lobby. Not in the room. I'll come down to the lobby.

She didn't know exactly how old Frederick was. About seventy, a miracle actually that he was still around; he could have been gone by now; that would have been more likely. She had phoned him. He had answered the phone. This startled her so much she almost hung up. His voice sounded low and soft. Not frail. But soft. She took a deep breath. Hello, my name is Alice, she said. We don't know each other, but I'm Malte's niece.

For a moment Frederick said nothing. Then he asked how she got hold of his phone number, his voice neither friendly nor unfriendly, matter-of-fact.

From the phone book, Alice had said. It was the truth.

In that moment, during which he said nothing, in that very short stretch of time, Alice knew that her call had forced Frederick to think back over almost forty years – whether he wanted to or not. Back through all the ups and downs, back to the day his friend Malte had taken his own life. Was that hard for him? With her phone call Alice had turned Frederick's day upside down, had ripped him out of whatever he was just then doing, out of the equilibrium of his everyday world. Thoughtless and needy. By reminding him of a name – pronounced as softly and gently as possible.

Oh, Frederick had said. And what's this all about?

Still, Frederick had said, Oh, and what's this all about, and Alice, grateful for the almost casual tone in his voice, had said that she didn't really know what she was hoping for, but she'd like to see him.

I'd like to meet you. That's all. I can't give you a good reason.

He seemed to understand that. Or it seemed to be all right with him. He asked, Do you live in Berlin? – He meant: Do you live in Berlin, just as Malte had lived in Berlin, even though, unlike Malte, you're obviously not dead – and Alice said, yes, she lived in Berlin, and as she was saying it, saw in her mind's eye the picture of a plant in a clay pot on the windowsill of a ground-floor apartment that looked out on a dark rear courtyard, on dustbins and carpet rods. All around the pot were the crunchy shells of insects. That's what came to mind. Who knows why.

Well, I still get to Berlin, Frederick said. Frequently. Let's meet in Berlin. Give me your phone number. I'll call you the next time I'm in Berlin.

He had set the conditions. His voice had suddenly become strong, alert. Alice gave him her phone number; he didn't repeat it. And it might have gone no further. But two months later he had actually called her.

Alice stumbled in her high heels, tripped, and was surprised by the brief jolt to her spine, an icy throbbing. She should have worn different shoes, should have left her shoulder bag at home. Her coat was already spotted from the rain and by the time she arrived, the right shoulder would be crumpled by her bag. Who was it she actually wanted to introduce to Frederick? Obviously not herself. Alice tipped back her umbrella and looked up into the black tree branches; her face got wet. The day was so grey that everything glowed: the orange of the refuse truck, the yellow of the mail trucks, the golden halos behind the fogged-up windows of the cafés. Roller shutters rattled. The bin men clanged dustbins into the entryways, as noisily as possible. From behind the scaffolding that covered the house facades came music from transistor radios, drowned out by an avalanche of construction debris. Fire-engine sirens, sounding a four-note interval, a helicopter hurtling across the sky with a deafening roar. Twilight. The temperature barely above freezing on this day in November. What is this all about? What's it all about? Alice might also have said, Frederick, you know, it's actually all about me. But she didn't say it, and she wasn't going to say it. Frederick would know anyway.

Alice hadn't known Malte. Malte would have been her uncle if he hadn't committed suicide on a day in March – almost forty years ago. Alice was born in April, one month later. But by the time her life began Malte was already lying under the green grass – stones, jasmine and rhododendron around his grave. You are the light in our darkness, Alice's grandmother, Malte's mother, had written on her calendar in a clear, deliberate hand.

Alice shook her head, clicked her tongue. To be the light in someone's darkness. She could see her car now. It was standing where she had parked it yesterday, next to the planetarium behind a row of shaggy forsythia bushes. She was always surprised to find her car exactly where she'd left it. There was a message clamped under the windscreen wiper. The bearer of the message was already ten cars away, a skinny gypsy in a black leotard. His shoulders were bare; his right leg dragged, and he was preaching at the top of his lungs – incomprehensible, full of rage or ecstasy, it could have been either. The dome of the planetarium was varnished with rain. Fat crows in the winter grass, and along the edge of the meadow, the clatter of the S-Bahn. Alice waited until the gypsy had turned the corner and disappeared into the new housing development. He was slow, limping from windscreen to windscreen, now and then looking up into the sky. Alice followed his gaze. Nothing to be seen. Rain clouds, dark as ink. When she looked back again at the row of cars, he was gone. On the little red plastic card under the wiper was the phone number of some stranger who was interested in buying Alice's car. Hurriedly and distractedly, she searched for her car key in her bag, opened the car door, put the little card on the passenger seat, her bag next to it, got in and slammed the car door shut, as usual much too hard. It was a Japanese car. Tiny, made of Japanese cardboard. Hanging on the rearview mirror, a dream-catcher – a web of string with brown and white feathers attached. Chewing-gum wrappers in the tray next to the gearstick. Tickets from parking meters, some coins, the smell of damp plastic – what an absolutely personal space. Something made the tears come to Alice's eyes, possibly it was only weariness. She inserted the key in the ignition, started the engine, and awkwardly manoeuvred the car out of its parking space. The gypsy had not returned. The windscreen wipers started up and, chirping softly, traced clean half-moons on the wet glass.

Alice knew that Malte didn't have a driving licence, in the late sixties in West Berlin. As far as she knew, he didn't know how to drive, may have wanted to learn, but never got round to it. Too much to do. He liked going to Prinzenbad, the public pool. Would lie around at the pool on Prinzen Strasse day after day in June, July, and August. Smoking, of course. Garbáty Kalif? Wearing check shirts, narrow trousers. Back then a ticket on the U-Bahn cost 50 Pfennig. Lovely 10-Pfennig coins in his trouser pocket, the ticket made of heavy paper. The U-Bahn ran above ground on Prinzen Strasse between the bullet-riddled grey buildings, then hurtled underground before it reached Wittenberg Platz, and only re-emerged into the light just before Krumme Lanke. Zehlendorf. Malte had lived in his mother's house in Zehlendorf. A three-storey house, lilacs, elderberry bushes, a porch in the back. When he was eighteen years old, Frederick was ten years older, and the war had been over for twenty years. The grass grew high, the dandelions too. The whole garden was overgrown with weeds. The name of the street was Waldhüterpfad. The U-Bahn station was called Onkel Toms Hütte. Reeds grew all around the edges of Krumme Lanke lake. There was a rowboat, called *Maori*. And a cat named Pumi in the tall grass, among the dandelions and juicy leaves of clover. Lemonade in scratched glasses. And such starry clear nights!

Malte had loved Frederick, and Frederick had loved Malte. That much Alice knew, a handful of words, and some sensory impressions – the smell of pine trees, lake water, and sun-warmed cat fur. That much she'd pieced together from the little they had told her. And they hadn't told her much. Worked it out from the photos – a cat in the grass, her rear legs stretched out, her little head facing the camera with a haughty cat expression, that certain feline all-knowingness, a snapshot in black and white. Beneath it, on the photographic paper, her grandmother had used a crayon to write: *Pumi*. A photo of Malte, smoking. Wearing a striped shirt, sitting on the porch, his hair hanging over his forehead, his eyes cast down, twenty years old. Three years later Alice was born. No photo of the lake, no photo of the boat. Alice knew the lakes and boats. The word Maori had a good sound, a nice sound. Kissing in the heat. Skin and hair. To think of only one man, feeling despair and delight.

Alice didn't know why Malte had taken his own life. She was surprised that nobody had been able to tell her why; they just looked at her in surprise, wide-eyed, when she asked. With faces like clowns. Well, there's no way to know. There's nothing to know. Depression, melancholy, manic-depressive psychosis? Tired of life. He was weary of life. But how could that be?

Alice drove her Japanese car down the narrow street, past the planetarium towards the main road, and was caught up in the morning traffic, her eyes half closed. The dream-catcher swung from side to side in slow motion, the coins rattled in the tray next to the gearstick. The traffic lights glowed. She had no idea why she'd phoned Frederick at this particular time. This year. In the autumn. Because he was getting older and older, just as she was. Because people were suddenly gone, vanishing from the scene from one day to the next. That's probably why. She had been thinking about him ever since she had first heard his name mentioned; he was part of Malte's story, but not part of the family; that was what made him stand out. He had some perspective. No one else did. Tidying up – it had something to do with tidying up, putting things in order, the desire to know which assumptions one could lay aside, and which ones not yet. To drop this particular assumption, and to look for another instead. To see connections, or to see that there weren't any connections at all. Just presumed relationships. Illusions, like reflections, nothing more than changes in the temperature, the light, the seasons.

She drove down the main road from the north-east towards the west, towards the compass-needle point of the TV tower. Traffic stopped and then slowly started moving again. Behind the window of a coffee shop, a woman took off her sweater, her braid catching in the collar; the blouse under the sweater was a faded pink; her legs were twisted around the struts of a bar stool. At an entrance gate a worker stopped the drum of a cement mixer and stripped off his gloves. The driver of a taxi parked at the kerb was sleeping, his head on his chest. Fallow land, garages with caved-in roofs, a petrol station, a plastic tiger swinging from steel cables. Convention hotels, tourist hotels, lofts. Behind the panoramic windows of factory buildings people were running on treadmills, their heads turned up to watch TV monitors, the pictures changing rapidly. Advertising billboards: Smoked Fish. Play your Heroes. Ubu Roi. Bang bang, the night is over. Black Maple. The grey-green trunks of plane trees. Crows or magpies, or jackdaws. Red lights. In the car next to Alice's, a woman was filing her nails, a cellphone clamped between her left ear and shoulder. Apparently she was saying a weary, slow goodbye, agitated, shifting gears, stepping on the gas. Then the woman turned off the main road, and Alice drove on towards the tall buildings of newspaper offices, the Haus des Lehrers, and the Haus des Reisens; a tram cut through the intersection, and a young woman who had taken shelter at the tram stop searched in the depths of her purse for something, something very small and apparently precious.

And Frederick. Frederick, meanwhile, was in his room at the hotel near the river. It was half an hour before his meeting with Alice, whom he didn't know, whom he had never before seen, and of whom he knew nothing all these years. What is it like for him? Alice wondered. Is it like a game, is it serious, or does none of it matter to him? It's possible he doesn't care about anything. Or that it interests him only a little. That's all.

She tried to imagine his hotel room, a single room with a wide, queen-size bed and an armchair at the window, a wine-red carpet, his overnight bag for short trips on the luggage rack and beside it, on a hook, his coat on a hanger, a sea-blue housecoat. Next to the door, framed in brass, a map showing the emergency exit routes in case of fire. You are here, a little red cross. True, in many ways. Signs to hang on the doorknob for the chambermaid: Do not disturb, Make up the room. Soundproof windows, a noisy air-conditioner. On the bedside table, a telephone next to the bedside lamp, a pad and pencil with the name of the hotel on them, and a piece of dark chocolate in a black and gold wrapper. I'll call once I'm in the lobby, Alice had said. Is that all right with you?

Eventually Malte had moved out of the Zehlendorf house, the one with the porch, the cat, and the dandelions. He lived by himself in a one-room apartment in Kreuzberg, on a street called Eisenbahn Strasse, Railway Street. Frederick was away, studying elsewhere; they exchanged letters, saw each other rarely. A nearly empty room, a bed, no table, no chair, a clothes rail, and hanging on it, a wire hanger with a blue shirt, a second hanger with a pair of black trousers. A cast-iron lamp, a tape recorder, reels of tape, a radio, a record player on the floor, and books stacked in crooked piles. File folders. A pair of dumb-bells. Photo albums, records. Malte's room, Malte, who, they said, showed a troublesome inclination towards ending it all – did the others say that? Or did he say that about himself? Alice wedged her car into the street by the river, without paying attention to any of the traffic signs, exhaled, and finally took her foot off the accelerator. Almost forty years ago, the janitor had to force the door to that room open with a crowbar because the key was in the lock on the inside and Malte had not answered his mother's persistent, fearful knocking. Once the door was open, it was too late. It was all over. All of this so long ago.

How did he kill himself? With painkillers, pills. Barbiturates – a word almost as sonorous as Maori. Back then you could still get barbiturates without a prescription, not any more, and that was all Alice knew. The end. That's as far as she could think. Delicate threads between her in her Japanese car in the no-parking zone outside the hotel, shoulderbag on her knees and fingertips on her throbbing eyelids, and Frederick in his room with the river view, waiting for the phone to ring, and Malte for whom there had been no one at the end to be a light in the darkness. Threads as fine as a spider's web, cut the moment she tried to think about it. Alice opened the car door and got out.

In her own room there was a picture leaning against the wall next to the window. An owl. Its wings spread before a whorl of shadows. It was a picture Malte had painted. She couldn't have said whether it was a good painting or not. That wasn't the point. Sometimes she would sit at the table and gaze at the owl. Involuntarily cocking her head to the side. Then she'd get up and do something else.

The golden hand of a train-station clock hanging above the hotel reception desk moved to the top of the hour. The smell of leather and furniture polish, peppermints in a glass bowl. Alice said, Hello, would you please ring Room 34, her left hand on the reception desk in an attempt to get some attention. Water dripped onto the floor tiles from her furled umbrella; she could hear it drip. The hotel clerk had a deformed ear; it was twisted and stunted; his hair looked as if it had been cut with nail scissors, but the name-plate on his lapel shone like filmed-over silver. He ignored Alice for a while, drawing lines and circles with a pencil in a big ledger, deadly earnest; Alice couldn't see exactly what he was doing. Two waitresses were clearing away the buffet in the breakfast room, aggressively clattering the plates, sweeping off the tables with hand brooms, collecting crumpled newspapers. Disorder, a restless atmosphere, coy giggles. The hotel clerk mumbled to himself, his head averted.

Would you do that please Alice said.

Of course, he said. Gently, with an expression of unlimited patience. As if he had just wanted to give Alice a little time, a small span of time, so that she could reconsider everything. Change her mind, retreat. Alice thought, But that's something I never learned to do. Sorry, that's not possible any more. She didn't smile, felt her left eyelid twitch; inconspicuously she withdrew her hand from the counter, leaving a damp mark that vanished as she watched. The clerk closed the ledger and put the pencil down next to it. He lifted the telephone receiver and, as if he were in a silent film, dialled a number and held the receiver out to her over the counter. Alice angrily rejected it, almost pushing away the hand extending the telephone to her, almost touching him.

Tell him Alice is here, she whispered. He raised his eyebrows, put the receiver to his good ear, and listened. No one there? Would someone have to break down the door? Did Frederick need a little more time so that he could change his mind about the whole thing? After all he'd had to learn to do without.

Alice knew that Frederick, sitting in the armchair next to the suddenly ringing telephone, must have flinched in shock. Even though he had been waiting for it to ring. Just because of that. The abrupt shock. His heart pounding, the theoretical acknowledgement of futility.

Alice is here, the clerk said. Almost pleading. He had been given the key word, knew the text. He nodded, listened some more, a pained half-smile on his lips. Then he replaced the receiver. Looking at Alice, looking right through her, he said, The gentleman is coming down to the lobby. Right away.

Alice didn't know where to go. She was standing in front of the elevator, in the middle of the lobby, the reception desk to her right and the breakfast room to her left. Circling the elevator were the stairs, a cabaret stairway with wide steps, the banister rail of dark wood and golden diagonal posts. Would Frederick take the elevator or the stairs? Either way he'd be making an entrance. The elevator was waiting on the fourth floor; the digital display above the elevator door remained steadily on the number 4. The lobby floor was paved with black and white tiles, freshly washed, showing distinctly the tracks left by Alice's shoes and her dripping umbrella. An old woman was pushing a cart full of wrinkled, soiled laundry past the reception desk down the long hall. Umbrellas swam by outside the windows; it seemed to be getting dark already. The hotel clerk yawned like a tired child. He undid the foil wrapper around a stick of chewing gum and pushed it into his mouth. Sucking on it thoughtfully. In the breakfast room the waitresses were crawling around on their hands and knees under the tables. They straightened tablecloths, flower arrangements, cinnamon sticks, and dried orange slices. They bumped their heads, pulled their braids tight with both hands.

Alice switched the bag from her right shoulder to the left, took the umbrella into her left hand. She thought of her grandmother who all her life had had a recurring dream in which she was in a large room, sitting at a festive table set only for her, in front of a tureen made of the finest porcelain. When she raised the lid, there in the white bowl was a black, multi-legged, unusually intricately equipped insect, stretching out and flicking up its shiny feelers. Tentacles. Tendrils like wire. In the autumn, Alice's grandmother liked raking the leaves of the nut trees, leathery leaves, the smell of earth and oil. Every other year, there would be nuts, shrivelled and plentiful; they would lie spread out on newspapers by the window, and at noon the sun would shine for an hour on their shrivelled husks. Her grandmother had supported the first small sunflower stems with paint brushes, tying the stems to the brushes with thread. When she came downstairs to the kitchen after her midday nap, her bronze bracelet clattered on the banister. She believed in the nerve-strengthening power of bananas. In the evenings she played Napoleon patience and, despairing when it didn't come out, would leaf through a French grammar book to compensate, rustling the yellowed pages until her eyes closed. Then she would feel for the switch inside the shade of the cast-iron lamp that had been her mother's and her mother's mother's before that and afterwards had been Malte's, and then again hers and now Alice's. Alice's grandmother had died in a hospital even though she had expressly asked to be allowed to die at home. In her last hour of life she had spoken steadily and insistently, but Alice hadn't understood a single word because the nurses refused to put her grandmother's teeth back in her mouth – saying she might have a convulsion and choke to death. That's how it was. Then, later, Alice was handed a plastic bag containing her grandmother's cardigan, a pair of shoes, and the bronze bracelet. She had turned down the offer to say goodbye to her one more time in the morgue the following day.

Her grandmother wouldn't have said anything about the meeting between Alice and Frederick. Neither for nor against it, not the one nor the other. Alice thought that her grandmother, in her old age, had been a happy person in a humble way. Frederick came down the stairs. An old man. Very fine hair, white, almost gleaming, and Alice realised with amazement that she had actually assumed he would be young. As young as he had been almost forty years ago. She had assumed Frederick had stopped ageing when Malte died. That his story had stopped at the point where hers began. She made an almost apologetic movement towards him, and Frederick let go of the banister on the last step and came towards her, his gaze focused attentively on Alice's face – and Alice knew that he would be disappointed at finding no external resemblance between her and Malte, not the least. On the other hand it was no longer possible to know what Frederick had looked like back then. On the porch. Light, shadow, and light, alternating on his features. But despite all that, they looked at each other. Shook hands and their touching was encouraging, it was what was left to them.

Well now, let's go outside for a bit, Frederick said. He had a slight squint. Sounded indulgent, and he smiled that way too. Good thing you brought an umbrella, he said.

They walked together along the river. The voices of the tourist guides on the excursion boats floated across the water, fragmented and windblown, ... *once stood here, used to be, will be and is today*. Frederick walked under the umbrella Alice held over him, every now and then sticking his face out into the rain. He was shorter than she was. They walked slowly. He was carrying a plastic bag with something in it. No coat over his blue suit. Alice thought he would dissolve if it weren't for the umbrella she was holding over him. Dissolve and run like watercolours, different hues of blue: marine, hyacinth, hydrangea. An express train roared across the bridge. Pigeons flew up. Signals. Departure and arrival. The river water lapped against the bulwark, carrying trash, paper and bottles. Building cranes swayed next to the Tränenpalast. Frederick said, This time I'd like to go to the Bode Museum. Back then, he paused, it wasn't possible. But I'm going there this afternoon. It was not an invitation for her to go with him.

They sat across from each other, the only customers in a dimly lit café, Alice drinking tea, Frederick too, no sugar, no milk. The waitress behind the counter was reading a book. At Frederick's request she had turned off the radio. An ice crystal was rotating with psychedelic slowness on the computer screen of the cash register. Now and then Alice gazed at Frederick, his white, feathery light hair, his reflective glasses, his skin dark and meticulously shaved, an expression of weariness and arrogance around the mouth. Also a childish look of hurt feelings. He had a problem with swallowing. Coughed frequently. His hands looked soft, carefully cut fingernails and a signet ring showing a rising or a setting sun.

Alice wondered what Malte would have looked like today. What sort of mood, what sort of shape would he be in. Her homosexual uncle. No children, unmarried. A long table of scarred wood, the smell of oil paints, turpentine, varnish, sticks of charcoal, hand-rolled cigarettes, pale, transparent cigarette paper as thin as tissue, and tobacco, black and dry. A slightly acrid smell that clung to his fingertips for a long time, the index and middle fingertips on his right hand tinted yellow. An inclination towards ending it all. He would have pushed aside the papers, cups, ashtrays, and sticks of charcoal to make room for her at his table. Alice thought, I would have gone to see him, lovesick. Would have picked up a short, cynical remark of consolation. An indication. And she realised with amazement that she missed Malte, that his departure had spread into her life, even if only as an illusion, a projection aimed almost into nothingness.

How is your father? Frederick asked. He spoke past Alice, through the window. Wait a minute – yes, yes, your father, Christian, Malte's brother.

He's well, Alice said automatically. He's well.

And Alice? He pronounced the name of Alice's grandmother as if he had forgotten that Alice had the same name. True. It wasn't the same. Not the same name.

Alice has been dead a long time already, Alice said. She stumbled inwardly, but only over the short, dry word. It wasn't as if she were talking about herself, it had never been like that. Her grandmother had been dead for almost twenty years. That was hard to believe; she had to repeat it. Alice died twenty years ago. But she wasn't sick for long. She felt fine, almost to the end.

I'm glad, Frederick said. She was very gentle. Your grandmother. A gentle, wise, and patient woman, extraordinarily patient, considering what a hard time she had. And not only with Malte.

Alice's grandmother had not been gentle. Or patient.

Those weren't the right words, not at all. But Alice didn't contradict him; she hadn't known her as Malte's mother. Had no image of the woman who walked out on the porch of the house on Waldhüterpfad in the mornings. The cat purring around her feet, its matted fur. Her grandmother's hands half a century ago. Her voice back then, Malte's voice, her gestures, the tender words, all the futile good intentions. When finally her sons were grown men, she got sick. Malte and Christian sold the house on Waldhüterpfad.

There was nothing left of all that. Only the picture of the owl, three chairs, the cast-iron lamp, a few records, the two dumb-bells for a while – and then those too were gone, swept away by something. What's it like? Alice asked her father every year as they passed the house on their way to the cemetery to place a candle in a red plastic container on the neglected grave. Every year they stopped at the house, and Alice would peer in at the window next to the front door, into the living room, past the furniture of strangers, and out to the rear of the garden, without understanding anything. To be allowed to sit on the porch just once. Just once. What is it like to stand outside the house in which you grew up, now that other people are living in it? Her father raised his hands. What can I say?

Does Christian know we're meeting? Frederick asked, at the same time signalling to the waitress. The waitress saw him out of the corner of her eye, got up, but not until she had finished reading the page she was on, only then did she close her book.

No, Alice said. No one knows. But not for any particular

reason; it's just that – this is my affair. It's my business. And Frederick nodded, that's how he felt too.

Well, then, the bill for the two pots of tea, please.

The waitress stood next to their table, not as if Frederick had signalled to her, but as if she had been assigned by someone else to put an end to their meeting. She held her waitress purse open in her left hand, having placed the right one protectively over her left wrist, covering her pulse. Out of politeness, Alice leaned down to get her shoulder bag, but Frederick paid for them both, leaving the correct tip. Scarcely looked at the waitress, not interested. The waitress snapped her purse shut with a flourish, rattling the coins. Well now, she said. Have a nice day, Hope the rain lets up.

I brought you something, Frederick said. It was a small, fat blue file folder that he had been carrying in the plastic bag. He put it on the table in front of him without opening it.

Malte's letters. These are the letters Malte wrote to me in the years before he died. You can read them. I think they'll tell you everything you might want to know. Actually everything is in those letters.

Yes. He looked at the blue folder as if he wanted to reconsider, then he slid the file folder back into the bag, pushed the bag across the table. Alice kept her hands in her lap.

The letters have been in a safe deposit box at the bank all this time. I'm getting old now, and I don't know when I might pass out and not regain consciousness or something, and I don't know who might find me then.

He got up, pushed the chair back against the table. His

voice sounded quite unemotional. He probably wanted it that way to make it all bearable.

He said, I'd like to have the letters back after you've read them.

They both knew this wouldn't happen.

I'll give them back to you, Alice said emphatically. Thanks.

She said, By the way, I was there once. I passed by there once.

Where, Frederick asked. Passed by what?

Eisenbahn Strasse 5, Alice said. The house where Malte lived in those days.

Really, Frederick said. And what was it like? He seemed to be truly interested, even if at some remove, from a safe distance.

It was strange, Alice said. How can I describe it – I was nervous; it was as if I were following someone. Spying on someone …

For quite a while she had stood across the street from the house, looking at it, an apartment house like all the others, from the 1870s, its facade renovated. She had thought about the fact that Malte had come and gone across that threshold for a whole year, and then walked in one last time and had not walked out again; they had carried him out, a sheet covering his body and his face. But she preferred imagining what it would be like if the front door were to suddenly open and he were to walk out, hands in his jacket pockets, casting an inquiring glance up at the sky. She wondered if she would recognise him and how – by the scar on his forehead, the protruding ears, old Alice's eyes, his posture in general. She was sure she would recognise him, and a wave of indignation and affection passed through her, even though the front door remained shut tight and no one left or entered. But it could have been possible. Anything was possible. Raymond might have come out of the house. Or the Romanian. Or Misha, who seemed more alive the longer he was dead; everything seemed to be connected with everything else, and from that perspective it wasn't surprising that the thing that glittered among the paving stones directly in front of the apartment house door should turn out to be an undamaged gold-coloured cartridge. Without looking to the left or to the right, Alice had crossed the street heading towards the front door, had bent down and picked the cartridge up out of the soft, sandy depression between two cobblestones. And put it in her pocket.

You know, she said, I suddenly had the thought that he didn't die at all. That all this time he's been living in the house on Eisenbahn Strasse, all these years. It's as if I'd finally found out something. Do you know what I mean?

Well, I can imagine it, at least, Frederick said.

There was a cartridge lying outside the front door, Alice said. A nine-millimetre Parabellum.

It's for you, Frederick said. Just like that, he said.

Yes, for me, Alice said. I wonder why.

You'll find out, Frederick said. You will find out.

Afterwards he walked across the bridge over the river, the brackish water the same today as back then, the iron Prussian eagles forged into the bridge railing by their wings. And nobody was watching. Except Alice, who watched him walk off, freed now from the burden of the little bag containing the letters Malte had written in those years. It had stopped raining. Frederick strolled off, stopped once and turned to look up at the building cranes. What was he thinking about? Then he walked on. It wasn't he who had phoned Alice. Alice had phoned him. Was there someone after Malte? Alice had asked him. No, Frederick had replied. After Malte there was no longer anyone, only some physical encounters, but that's something quite different. It seemed he didn't think it remarkable that there was no one else after Malte.

A flatbed pickup truck was coming out of the narrow street of the hotel where the clerk handed room keys attached to heavy brass weights across the counter to new hotel guests, where the waitresses took off their aprons in the laundry room, brushing their hair in the light of fluorescent tubes. The pickup truck, turning with deliberate speed out of the narrow street on the eastern bank of the river, was carrying Alice's Japanese cardboard car. With its dream-catcher, petrol receipts, hair clips, broken umbrellas, picnic blankets, old newspapers, sand from Lake Müritz, peanut shells, sweet wrappers, and aspirin. On the passenger seat the little plastic card from the gypsy who – on the periphery of the new housing development – had looked up into the sky, the way Frederick had, and then had disappeared, vanished, never to reappear. Alice watched the pickup truck. She had a brief, feeble impulse to run after it but tripped again in her high heels.

Gripping the bag containing Malte's letters, she walked up the stairs to the train station. And now what? Read the letters right away or later or not at all? It didn't matter what was in them – it wouldn't change anything. But it would add something – one more ring around an unknowable permanent centre. Alice tightened her hold on the bag of letters. I am, after all, one of many, she thought, losing herself in the splendid, cold and wintry hall of the train station among so many others, and all the many possibilities of travelling here or there.

V

Raymond

After Raymond died, Alice began getting rid of his things. Putting away, giving away, throwing away, selling. Keeping. A kind of excavation project, uncovering the layers, the various colours, materials, eras; in the end there would be nothing to salvage, nothing except for the fact that Raymond was dead. That's what it boiled down to. It wasn't the worst of jobs.

She started with his jackets. It just turned out that way, pure coincidence; maybe she should have started with something else, but in the end it probably didn't matter. The jackets were hanging in the hall, over the back of a chair in the living room, and on a brass hook, or downstairs in the cellar on nails hammered into the door. She started with those in the living room. A green one and a blue one. The green one made of water-repellent nylon, the blue one of a soft cotton material with a removable lining; without the lining it was very light. Alice hesitated a moment; then she did what she had wanted to do all along, maybe just to see what it would be like. She knew it was actually senseless because the entire apartment still had Raymond's smell, particles of his skin and his hair; besides, it was a cliché from the movies, from books: Picking up the blue jacket with both hands, she buried her face in the soft fabric, but the fabric smelled of the apartment, of dust, of home, and of a particular detergent, and that was all, nothing else. Raymond had worn that jacket one afternoon a hundred years ago, in the spring, sitting outside the employment office on a bench next to a snack bar on a side street. A wooden kiosk, blue and white painted laths, a window in the middle of which was an opening, the glass completely blocked by a display of schnapps bottles, cigarette cartons, fizzy-drink cans. Music from a radio. Popular songs from the fifties, a weather forecast, jokes, and traffic reports. The penetrating smell of frying fat came through the opening. In front of the kiosk, some men, their dogs tied to the lamp post, were standing around an empty barrel, beer bottles in hand, snapping their braces and spitting. One of them was talking. The others, all listening. When the time came to laugh, they all laughed, one man laughing the loudest; the dogs barked like crazy; then, frightened, they stopped. Thorny bushes on both sides of the bench. Alice and Raymond had been sitting there next to each other. Alice was drinking coffee out of a plastic cup, Raymond had a beer. The weather hadn't really warmed up yet, but the sky was already quite blue, radiantly white clouds chasing each other. Raymond had rolled himself a cigarette and looked at Alice. Nothing more. That look at Alice was perfect as long as it lasted. That was all.

Alice carefully folded the blue jacket. In the right pocket she found a spare part for the car, a tiny boomerang made of fine, stamped metal, shrink-wrapped in a little plastic bag, brand new. Daihatsu Cuore. She weighed it in her hand, then she put it on the table.

She put the blue jacket into the box headed for the attic. The green jacket was an aviator jacket with silver epaulettes, an American logo. Raymond had worn it once on a walk they took through the Botanical Garden. In the summer. He had said, sounding doubtful, Looks too good, or something. Alice had to laugh. They were both stoned, it was very long ago, walking arm in arm on a pebbled path past the silhouettes of the satellite towns at the edge of the garden, and they saw guards in the distance coming towards them, muzzled Alsatians on a short leash. They'd turned around then; the garden was locked after they left. Later they went to the cinema.

Which film?

Forgotten. A different memory.

It occurred to Alice that she apparently couldn't choose the memories; they came of their own accord: the memory of the garden, Raymond in the aviator jacket – soundless and yet part of it all. Later Alice had worn the jacket occasionally. Looks too good, or something. She pulled up the zipper, put the jacket into the box for the Red Cross.

She added the jackets from the cupboard in the hall without stopping or checking any of the pockets. A scarf, two hats, everything into the box, one after the other. Everything.

But in one of the jackets from the cellar she found something she was utterly unprepared for – even though she'd tried to be prepared for everything. It was something small, it was almost as if Raymond had left it for her – a crumpled paper bag from a bakery containing the remnant of a little almond horn. The curved end of the little crescent, so old as to be almost petrified. And like a shell in a fossil, a smooth almond sliver on top.

Alice, standing there in the dim light of the cellar, the bag in one hand, the remains of the crescent in the other, shook her head. Whether she wanted to or not. Through the open cellar door, the childish chatter of the Indian cooks came floating down the cellar steps, the kitchen door slamming, propane gas cylinders rolling across the stone floor of the hallway, she could even hear the buzzing of the fat flies down here. The smell of the dustbins in the courtyard drifted down into the cellar, mixing with the cellar smell, the sharp odour of rat poison, mould, and damp bricks.

Raymond. He'd been hungry – a simple, lively hunger. Had bought himself an almond horn at that one particular bakery. Must have been on a Tuesday, Wednesday, Thursday, Friday, or Saturday. Sunday and Monday this bakery was closed, and the fact that it was closed on Mondays was for Raymond proof of its quality. Like the old days. It was winter – the bag was in a pocket of his winter jacket along with a glove. Where was the other glove? And had Alice been there at the time? Was she there when Raymond bought the little almond horn? Did he break off a piece for her, giving it to her or putting it in her mouth – at midday, in the afternoon, or in the morning of a cold and windy day while they were walking along next to each other, Alice's arm in Raymond's arm, and her hand shoved into his glove together with his. Some more? No thanks, and the last piece back into the bag. Raymond had dropped the last piece back into the bag, twisted it shut, and put it into his jacket pocket. When? Or had he been by himself, without Alice at his side; that also happened. And what to do with it now? A rising sun was printed on the paper bag. Good Morning. What to do with the rest, where to put it – that was something you had to learn.

Alice put the bag into the pocket of her own jacket. She just couldn't throw it away. There seemed to be a structure to these actions, time that had to pass. First find it, then comprehend it, then throw it away. Achieve a certain distance. Take your time – it annoyed her when Raymond used to say that. Take your time. Back upstairs. She put the winter jacket into the box for the Red Cross. The glove too. A glove for the right hand. She didn't slip her hand into it again.

And his shirts. His trousers. Underwear, T-shirts, hats, and shoes. A red and white checked shirt – no memories. A blue shirt brought a flood of memories, but she was able to push them away; she was able keep at bay the memory of Raymond opening the door for her one day in July, the middle of summer, one of innumerable record-breakingly hot summers – Raymond, very busy, had gone back into the apartment right away but was happy she had come. His face, the way his face looked when he was delighted to see her. She'd had a glass of tea, sitting by the window, leafing through a newspaper. Will you read to me? Nothing important. Raymond was wearing that blue shirt, little holes in it, carefully mended with many stitches, a round, old-fashioned neckline, as if from another time. So this was the shirt, then. And grey, green, or black trousers. Holes at the knees. Paint stains, torn pockets, decent trousers. Precisely folded T-shirts. With or without pictures printed on them. A silly bear. Camouflage patterns. Colourful prints. And Raymond's shoes. His orthotics. No glasses. Swimming trunks. Don't hesitate, Alice thought, trembling, Stop hesitating so idiotically long; and she put everything away, put all of it together and into the Red Cross box; the blue jacket and a green T-shirt were still in the box intended for the attic.

She carried the Red Cross box down the stairs. The box, the first of many, was pretty heavy. She had taped it shut with adhesive tape; no one would ever be able to get the tape off. Downstairs, the Indian cook came out into the hallway. An incredibly dirty apron. Chicken curry. Behind him, Alice could see the second Indian cook, against the red tiles, in the steam of the dishwasher. Nice pictures. Moving? The cook already looked shocked.

No, not moving. Throwing out, sorting, giving away, back into the stream.

Oh yes, the Ganges. The cook gave a loud laugh. Alice had to laugh too. He took the box from her and carried it the entire block to her car. He was wearing flip-flops, and he had brought the chicken curry smell with him from the kitchen. Also the smell of fresh-sliced pineapple, basil, tomatoes, and vinegar cleanser. That smell clung to the box and the car and Alice's hands until she dropped the box into the maw of a Red Cross container.

That first summer without Raymond she stalwartly went to the swimming pool. Almost every morning of every day she had off. And because she didn't want to drive out to the lake by herself – was unable to drive there by herself with the picnic blanket for her alone, the rustling of the newspaper pages, and the impenetrable thicket of the forest, it was hopeless. So, off to the swimming pool, maybe a more civilised thing to do. A short stretch on her bike on the shady side of the street, almost 20 degrees at nine o'clock in the morning. To the same swimming pool near the park that Raymond went to as a child – Alice had a photograph of Raymond on the steps in front of the changing cabins, six years old, squatting on the wet stone, one leg drawn to his chest, the other stretched out. He was squinting at the camera, against the light, and his black and white child's face was distorted because he was dazzled by the sun; yet Alice always thought that it looked as if he were crying. Raymond claimed he wasn't crying, that he had been jumping off the ten-metre diving board for an hour, constantly, without interruption; he had done that and then he'd gone home.

The stairs in front of the changing cabins were now blocked off. The paint on the broad steps was peeling, turquoise flakes; grass grew in the cracks between the stones. The spot where Raymond had been sitting back then was unrecognisable. But the diving board was in use today as it had been then, and swimmers were diving off the springy ten-metre board non-stop, a falling figure every three minutes. Alice spread out her towel near the large pool, next to a low wall behind which broom was growing and rubbish was piling up. Coffee cups, broken water wings, cigarette butts. She swam for half an hour, conscientious, neat lengths, her head held high above the water; then she walked back to her towel, stretched out on her back, closed her eyes. Planes. Sparrows in the broom, excited chirping. The ecstatic screaming of children and the quick steps of their little wet feet. Mothers spread out bath towels next to Alice, a dark shadow on her closed eyelids, as though a large bird were crossing the sky; then again the steady brightness, children, their teeth chattering, shaking the water from their hair, a shower of drops on Alice's stomach, like a human touch, something intimate.

Would you move over a little, please?

Alice, who was by herself with her small towel, her newspaper, and yellow bottle of suntan lotion, ranked lowest here; she accepted that and always smiled, grateful just to have someone speak to her. She rolled up her towel, moved aside, making room for more mothers with pushchairs, toting melons like cannon balls, pop bottles, Thermoses, mountains of folding chairs and plastic bowls full of pasta salad. Ensconced in this dreamlike atmosphere, she fell asleep. Shrill voices, laugher, children crying, the smell of peaches, tropical oils and wet stone, chlorine and the fine, dry smoke of cigarettes. And falling asleep she forgot that Raymond had died, forgot that he no longer existed, simply stopped thinking exhausting, wordless, terrible thoughts about him. She let go. Drifted away into the noonday heat, for one whole precious hour. Last night I dreamed that my teeth were falling out, a woman next to Alice was saying. It's supposed to have something to do with repressed sexuality. Oh, I don't believe it, said another, adding, as though that had settled it, It's a beautiful day.

I have to tell Raymond about that, Alice thought, sleepy and amused. I have to imitate the tone of her voice, the self-assured disparagement, followed by the casual remark about the weather. Then she remembered that this was no longer possible, and she came back to reality, wide awake, sat up as though someone had called her. She rubbed suntan lotion on her shoulders, legs, feet, and sat there a little while longer, holding the insides of her arms up to the sun. It had been a long time since she'd last sunned herself like this. The last time, probably a hundred years ago, when she'd been at Lago di Garda with Anna, really long ago. It was an aching, longing memory, a loving one – a state of being – nothing about this love would ever change. Anna's hair, dulled by the sun, her eyes, shiny black, rough hands like a child's. Lying next to each other, sunning themselves, just talking, looking out over the water, hands cupped over their eyes, rummaging among the water-worn pebbles, picking out a few but then leaving them behind. In the evening, checking out their tans in the mirror, the white breasts above the brown stomachs. She certainly hadn't done that with Raymond.

At midday Alice packed up her things, put her dress on over her bathing suit, and said goodbye to the mothers. They didn't reply, probably just out of laziness. Then she left. Passing the pool with the fountains where boys were dunking girls in the water, again and again pushing them down, then at the very last moment pulling them up by their hair, and the girls flew out of the water and screamed, triumphant and shrill. What kind of ritual was that? Alice was sure she and Raymond had also performed this ritual, long ago, both alone and with others, but she couldn't remember exactly. By the time she met Raymond, almost all the rituals had already been performed, almost all, except for just a few. Who would have thought? She dipped her feet into the lukewarm water of the shallow pool just before she came to the dried-up lawn, then put on her sandals.

Men with gold teeth were playing cards, under sun-bleached umbrellas in front of the kiosk where Raymond as a child had bought ice cream in a soft waffle, chocolate-coated vanilla wrapped in silvery foil. Tattoos, anchors on chains and hearts pierced by daggers, faded blue: For ever and ever. Naked people were sunning themselves on the lawn. Lying around singly under the white sky like people who'd been shot dead. Nothing was moving, except a threatening cloud of mosquitoes above a puddle at the end of the path, and the red and white barrier tape rattling between the trees in an imperceptible breeze.

Alice pushed her bike home through the afternoon streets. Some days she would push it all the way; she had the feeling that she was in danger and had to watch out and take care of herself, too tired from the heat and too deeply preoccupied to ride a bike – she thought, if I ride I'll have an accident, fly over the handlebars, and be run over, break my neck, break all my bones.

Take care of yourself.

You too.

And so she didn't ride. Bought strawberries at the corner from a stand shaped like a giant fruit. It had a green plastic stem on the roof, and in the shade inside were mountains of glowing strawberries in cardboard boxes stacked into pyramids. No, not a whole kilogram, thanks. Only half a kilo strawberries for Alice alone. She carried the berries home in a transparent bag. Locked the bike to the rack in front of the house. Since Raymond's death she no longer kept it in the courtyard. It was too much trouble, and she'd done it only for his sake; he thought the bicycle was safer in the courtyard.

The hallway was stifling. The apartment, quiet. Alice washed the strawberries long and thoroughly, letting the cold water run over her wrists, her rapid pulse. She cut the berries in half, then into quarters, sugared them, added a shot of vinegar, and put the bowl into the refrigerator. The blue flowers on the windowsill extended their austere, sturdy little petals – thirteen on each stem – towards the sun, impassive but purposeful.

Alice changed the beds. One sheet, two pillowcases, two blankets. She put on a fresh duvet cover. Crisp and cool the first night. She didn't dream that her teeth were falling out. Or that new ones would grow in their place.

She went to visit Margaret. Driving her car out of the city to the house-with-garden where Margaret now lived. A house in the suburbs, decentralised in many respects. They sat next to each other on the porch made of tropical wood and gazed at Margaret's flowers, the luxurious splendour of her flower beds: snapdragons, hydrangeas, and columbine, Japanese lilies.

Acqua Alba. The sky was blue, the planes were flying elsewhere. In the distance, the summer sounds of lawn-mowers, water sprinklers, the clatter of hedge shears. A cat came noiselessly onto the porch, sneezed dryly, settled down in front of them, straightening her front legs, and turning sideways, showing them her cat profile.

Cats do that, Margaret said. With two people they always position themselves so as to form an equilateral triangle. They always do that.

Alice looked at the cat, its reddish brown fur; the white spot at the end of the tail twitched slightly. Malte, Fred-erick, Pumi. It was reassuring to put everything she had together in her mind, put it together and see what the result would be.

And how to go on from there? Even with all the exhaustion – it was after all still early. The first days and weeks and months without Raymond – the days would never again be this clear and luminous; maybe she would have to learn how to find pleasure in it; any other way was impossible.

Richard said I would need three years, Margaret said. Just like that, he said it, imagine that. You'll need three years, then things will be easier for you.

And is it true? Alice asked.

No idea, Margaret said. A year has passed now, only one year, I'm far from understanding how he meant it. Three years. Would you like to take a few flowers home with you?

Yes, I'd love to, Alice said.

The lawn had been mown. Alice stood in the grass, barefoot. Margaret walked along the flower beds with a pair of scissors. Dahlias, sunflowers, and one thistle stem. The lawnmowers were silent now, wasps hummed around their nest in a pine tree. Cold orange juice. A wind sprang up, the porch door slammed shut, flat clouds in the sky.

Later on Alice went inside. Walking on the light-coloured tiles. Past the bookshelf on which stood a black and white photo of Richard. Taken in front of the bookshelf on Rheinsberger Strasse.

After that she gave away her car. It was quite clear that she had to give it away. It was too expensive, she couldn't afford it now that she was by herself; she used it far too rarely. Without Raymond, in fact, she didn't drive anywhere, and she didn't have to pick him up any more or take him somewhere; she'd stay put now. For that the bicycle and tram were adequate. She placed an ad in a car magazine, filling out the form in capital letters. Year: '87. Colour: red. Small dent on offside bumper. Windscreen slightly scratched. She worded it as best she could, and at the end thought up a price, not knowing whether it was appropriate or not. It seemed fair to her. Any price. What should it cost? It didn't matter.

The telephone began to ring in the middle of the night, at four a.m. Alice was lying on her back in bed, listening to the voices on the telephone answering machine, their graphic statements, foreign accents, thrice-repeated phone numbers, feverish promises. Requests to call back. Somewhere in the city all these people were wide awake. Busy. They had plans and were carrying out intentions. They had goals. She couldn't get herself to pull the plug out of the wall. Towards morning the phone stopped ringing. Quiet. Alice fell asleep. The first ball bounced against the fence of the basketball court. In the courtyard the wind rustled heavily in the trees.

At noon she walked to the car, carrying a blue bin bag and wearing sunglasses. Tropical temperatures. People were sitting in a row in front of the cafés in the semi-shade of the awnings; butter melting on their plates. Market stalls stood huddled at the edge of the park; the sun beat down on the cobblestone pavement. Cherry time. The last of the strawberries. Someone full of confidence had planted beans in the dust-dry soil surrounding the locust trees. Her car was parked at the planetarium. Alice unlocked the car door. Half-kneeling on the passenger seat, she opened the glove compartment and pulled out everything in it. Everything. Raymond's matchbooks, a chemist's calendar, petrol receipts, advertising leaflets. His supermarket discount coupons, other coupons. A creased photo of a chair standing next to a birch tree in front of a collapsed factory building. Ruins. Some sort of object on the ground next to the chair; Alice squinted, staring at the photo, but couldn't make out anything. She wouldn't be able to make out anything tomorrow either, or the day after tomorrow, not ever. Into the blue bag went the photo. Everything else too. And then among all the scraps of paper, suddenly – it could happen that quickly – she saw the plastic card, a green laminated card. Not the one from the gypsy back then, ages ago, but another one; still, they were probably all the same anyhow. *I am interested in your car. Now or later. Anytime. Give me a call. I'll be right over.* Alice crawled out of the car, whipped open the boot lid, stuffed everything that was in the boot into the blue bag. The picnic blanket – a colourful tartan, frayed at the edges, some of last autumn's leaves still in its folds. Hellsee. Or Lanke. Müritz. Water bottles, into the bag. An umbrella, the Thermos flask actually had something in it, some ancient liquid, probably tea made of leaves that Raymond had held between his fingertips. Holy, holy. Should she drink it? She dropped the flask into the blue bag and could hear the glass inside it breaking, a delicate splintering.

Was that all?

That was all.

The dream-catcher hung on the rear-view mirror, lashed to it.

Alice took her cellphone out of her bag, punched in the number on the card. Her hands were shaking, she didn't really know why. She said, I'd like to give away my car, please come and get it, yes, exactly, thanks, that would be very kind. She sat down on the kerb and waited. The car key in her hand, attached to it a metal token with a series of numbers stamped into it that must have had something to do with Raymond's life, but she had forgotten exactly what. Blocked synapses. She thought hard. Sitting motionless so that the jackdaws came quite close, their gleaming black wings, eyes, blunt beaks – little dinosaurs, absolutely indestructible.

She saw Raymond daily. Every day. She saw him everywhere; it was amazing how many manifestations, physical shapes he must have had – he could be everyman. He was standing on one of the escalators at the main railway station, moving through the high-ceilinged hall, a lightweight suitcase in his hand, his face in half profile, a traveller who was not in a hurry. Alice pushed someone aside and hurried through the hall, saw him step off the escalator, stroll over to the exit; it wasn't him, it was someone else. Her heart jumped with indignation because she saw him in the last carriage of a departing tram, at the traffic light on the other side of the street, in the queue at the supermarket; he got out of a taxi, lay sleeping on a park bench, rode a bicycle round the corner. He was sitting in an Italian ice-cream parlour, a dish of gorgeous fruit before him; an old man with dim eyes who saw Alice looking through the window, and shooed her away with his hand as if she were an animal. They were all Raymond. The way he walked, stood still, touched the back of his neck with his hand, rubbed his head, threw his shoulders back, yawned, put on his jacket, walked away. He isn't here any more, Alice, Alice told herself, addressing herself by her name as though she were her own child. Alice, Raymond isn't here any more.

What mattered was to preserve his memory, without going crazy in the process. To think of him without going crazy or becoming angry. Carefully. Over and over again. Starting from the beginning.

Where's your husband? the Indian cook asked.

Travelling, Alice said.

Oh really, for a long time? the Indian cook asked. He was sweeping the kitchen floor; the second Indian cook was sitting on an overturned bucket by the damp wall next to the dishwasher; his glasses were fogged up, he was smoking. Arabic music was coming out of a transistor radio, and he was beating time to it with his key chain, in restless, exact syncopation. Alice was leaning against the door to the hallway. The threshold was slippery. The Indian cook swept parsley stems, tomato halves, onion peels, rubber bands into a heap. Quitting time. He was humming to himself, then he put the broom down and drank apple juice from a bottle, taking large gurgling swallows. The day before, the second Indian cook had poured a bottleful of mineral water over his head in the middle of the kitchen, just like that. He didn't do it for Alice, but in spite of that Alice had enjoyed it.

Oh yes, for a long time, Alice said. It was impossible to say anything else. It was impossible to say, Raymond is dead. She had said that to the waitress, the tattooed one, in front of the house, on the street.

Where's your husband?

My husband is dead.

The tattooed waitress had said, My heartfelt condolences, yes, my heartfelt condolences; then she gave notice, moved somewhere else; nobody had ever written *Happy Hour* on the board as beautifully and clumsily as she.

Raymond is dead.

Alice couldn't say it again. Couldn't call it out into the kitchen. A draught of air, the aroma of parsley, a plastic tub with shimmering slices of lemon on a bed of ice, heads of lettuce on a wet wooden board, grapes, bananas, honeydew melons, dishrags, canisters of oil, huge glass jars of honey, tubs, and pots. Shortly before midnight. The second Indian cook crushed his cigarette out on the tiles. Took off his steamed-up glasses, cleaned them thoroughly, and put them back on. Still listening, his eyes rolled up, his twitching fingers shaking the bunch of keys, striking the bucket with the key ring, he mumbled something, thought for a while, then he yawned, got up, and with his foot pushed the bucket into a corner. He threw the keys up into the air, caught them, whistling softly; he turned round, extended his hands to Alice. The keys were gone.

Where to, said the first Indian cook.

On a trip.

He puffed out his cheeks, looked at Alice, leaning on the

broom handle as if it were a sceptre. Alice looked past him; she didn't know what to say in reply.

But the Indian cook said, I understand, I understand. Ah yes. I understand. He nodded steadily. Then he pointed at the second Indian cook and said: Four Eyes. Sees more than anyone else. Also going on a trip soon.

Where to, Alice said.

Oh, we'll see, the Indian cook said. Home? Back home maybe. Mumbai. Or to the moon.

Evenings at the table in their kitchen where Raymond used to sit, his elbows propped up in the invisible indentations that they must have left in the soft wood of the tabletop. Sitting there and watching as the blue flowers on the windowsill rolled up all their thirteen petals when the time came and their day's work was done. Day in, day out. The spiders that had hatched in the webs between the flower stems had grown, got big, some disappeared, others came into the apartment. Inside. Alice sat on a chair between the table and the cupboard and watched the spider that had set itself up in the corner above the kitchen door, probably for quite some time to come. Raymond would have removed the spider from the kitchen; she would have asked him to. But this spider would stay. Alice's grandmother would have approved. Alice whispered. Watching the spider spin its web and listening to the sounds in the courtyard. Water splashing, lengthy teeth-brushing. A telephone rang. Doors slammed shut. Footsteps on the stairs. The Indian cooks stamped on cardboard boxes, ripped paper into strips, stuffed the strips into the dustbins; then they smoked a cigarette together, and the smoke rose in the courtyard, all the way up to Alice who quietly went to sit on the window-sill. Late at night bats swooped down. And, of course, there were the last planes.

What was left was lying on the table. The replacement part for the car, the bag with the remainder of the almond horn. Nothing was left. The half-full box that had the jacket in it, the T-shirt, and the odds and ends stood next to Misha's suitcase which Maja had not yet picked up and which, whenever Alice lifted it, seemed to have got heavier as though there was something in it that kept growing. Since that time she had not looked inside. Alice knew that Lotte had tacked a little piece of paper next to her front door on which Conrad, when he was still alive, had written in a hurried and confident hand:

Be back soon.

Alice searched for something similar for herself and Raymond. Couldn't find it, but was certain that it existed. One day she would surely find it, probably by accident.

Sometimes Alice went to see the Romanian. She hadn't seen him for a long time, which was no problem, didn't seem to be a problem. Yet who knows, Alice thought, you find out about that sort of thing only later. The Romanian had grown older too, grey hair at the temples and thinner in a worrisome way, but his jug-handle ears still glowed unscathed. And he drank beer just as he always used to do and hadn't taken up smoking again, saying, I'll do that later on, when my last days come.

You can't choose the time, Alice said, amazed at so much ignorance. You can't know when your last days will be.

She tapped him lightly on the arm with her fist, and he smiled and moved aside. They were sitting on the balcony. You can sit here from nine o'clock in the evening until four in the morning, the Romanian said, then it gets too hot. Thirty degrees in the shade. Look at my plants – a regular biotope, wild clover and primeval mallows. He plucked at things in the flower boxes, pulled at some stalks, pointed at flower petals the size of a match head. Look at that. The prototype of a pansy.

Alice looked. A little cat face. She drank some water, the Romanian was drinking wine. The sun sank lazily. Then the half-moon rose. The sky, far away at the TV tower, above the Marienkirche and the neon sign of the Forum Hotel, was black. There won't be any thunderstorms, the Romanian said, clicking his tongue and nodding knowingly. Not until the full moon. It's the same as back home in Romania – a great open plain with lots of sun, no water, but apple trees in spite of that; shade under the apple trees, chickens running around, scratching in the soil, raising a little dust and so forth; and everything's still, holding its breath, waiting, and then suddenly there's a thunderstorm and the rain roars down on the plain and washes everything away. That's how it goes, but we're not there yet.

I'm hungry, Alice said, would you make me a sandwich?

Of course, the Romanian said, left and came back with a wooden board on which there were two open-face red-cherry jam sandwiches. My mother's jam. Watch out, you're dripping.

Alice ate the sandwiches, carefully and thoughtfully; it seemed as if she were eating a piece of bread with cherry jam for the first time in her life; the jam was so sweet, it made her mouth pucker – fruit and sugar. Tears came to her eyes. They looked down on the city, bare land, that was where the Wall had been, now sheep were grazing there, a warehouse, then the new buildings of the West; the first lights came on in the windows. All of it looked like a stage setting. Placed there. An installation. An aeroplane scraped diagonally past the moon. The S-Bahn came rolling in from the right, leaning heavily into the curve, a wonderful cadence on the rails. Wave to me if you should ever go by, because I'll be able to see it from here, the Romanian said.

I will, Alice said, I promise.

They didn't talk about Raymond. The Romanian didn't ask about Raymond, and Alice didn't mention him. Raymond hadn't cared much for the Romanian, maybe he'd been jealous, maybe he knew something or guessed or had a suspicion. The last shall be the first? Or the first shall be the last? But there was nothing to know. And there wouldn't be.

They didn't talk about any of the other things either. Actually, Alice realised that they were talking right past these things; possibly they were both too exhausted or couldn't decide whether they should. Whatever. She was glad it was this way.

Misha's child is doing well, the Romanian said at one point; she's growing up in the cemetery.

How do you know, Alice said.

I heard, the Romanian said casually. She plays in the cemetery, at Misha's grave. Her mother is always there. It's actually quite pleasant at the cemetery. In this weather. Nice and shady.

Yes, Alice said. Shady and cool.

The street lamps went on an hour before midnight. The climbers at the artificial rock wall next to the sheep meadow slowly roped down in wide arcs. Scissor-cuts. They made no sound. Crumpled moths tumbled into the light cast by the street lamps. Lightning bugs, the Romanian said. Alice knew that wasn't right.

If you stay a little longer you'll be able to see the space station. It passes by here, from back there; he pointed up and to the left, up into the black sky. And Mars, Saturn, Jupiter – they'll show up too. Believe me.

How does that old saying go? Alice asked.

Which saying?

The saying we used to remember the planets by when we were children. My very enthusiastic mother just served us, and so on and so forth.

You must know it, the Romanian said. I recited it for you many times.

Say it again anyway.

My very enthusiastic mother just served us noodle pudding.

They said it together, Mercury, Venus, Earth, Mars, Jupiter, Saturn, Uranus, Neptune, and Pluto. It doesn't apply any more, the saying, that is, the Romanian said. I hope you know that Pluto's been disposed of. In its stead there are now two other planets.

I know, Alice said. We could think up a new saying.

Later on she went home. Through a very friendly night. She continued to wave for quite a stretch without turning round, watching her shadow on the street, a distinct shadow, sharply outlined, the waving hand much daintier than her own. She knew that the Romanian, standing on his balcony, would be waving back until she had turned the corner. Goodbye. She walked past the closed cafés where the chairs were stacked and leaning against the tables, along the edge of the park towards the apartment house where she continued to live and where she had left the light on in the room on the third floor. All around the park, the smell of grass. Raymond was sitting in front of the house. On the step leading to the front door, his back against the wall, calm and waiting. Surprisingly, he was smoking; Alice could see the glowing tip of his cigarette. She walked a little faster, crossed the intersection, her shoes clattering on the cobblestones; the figure at the front door got up, and Alice wasn't disappointed when she saw that it wasn't Raymond at all, but the second Indian cook.

Four Eyes. In the end, a magician too. In his own way.